Out of the Embers

SP Neeson

Happy Reading ☺

SPx

18 STREET PRESS

Out of the Embers

A Glamour Blind Story

Copyright © 2024 by SP Neeson

www.18streetpress.com

Cover Designed by Natasha Snow Designs
www.natashasnowdesigns.com

Editing by Tracy Thillmann

ISBN: 978-1-7389875-8-0

Version: April 2024

For Kim – for being the greatest reader an author could ask for

And for Ryan – always

NOTE FROM THE AUTHOR

Hello Happy Reader! Before you begin, I must issue a warning. If you are here and have not yet read *Truth in the Smoke* and *Destiny in the Flames*, the first two books of the Glamour Blind Trilogy, you may want to pause and read those first.

It is possible to read this book without having read those. It should still make sense on its own. However, there are a couple of major spoilers in this book if you haven't read those ones yet. I strongly recommend you read the books in order for optimal reading pleasure.

But I can't tell you what to do. If you don't care about spoilers, read on. You have been warned.

Chapter 1

Ronan came down the stairs, and I made sure my glamour was in place before moving to intercept him. He didn't notice me right away, focused ahead on where he was going. Calynn and her entourage spent so little time at her Winter estate where I'd basically been kept prisoner for the last two weeks. Now was the first chance I had to enact my plan.

I moved forward—dressed in Calynn's clothes, with glamour turning my eyes from blue to silver—and walked right into him, exaggerating my stumble as I started to fall.

As I'd hoped would happen, Ronan caught me.

"Oh, Ronan. I didn't see you there."

He set me back on my feet with a polite smile. "No harm done."

His hands were already sliding away from my arms. I thought he would want her more than that; the way he was always looking at her certainly made it seem like he would. I thought he would take advantage of her practically throwing herself at him. But I had to catch his hand before he could let me go.

"Ronan," I said. "Let's not fight this anymore."

The smile immediately left his face, and I knew he wasn't fooled. Where had I miscalculated? My gift for glamour was better than most of the fae's. He should not be able to tell the difference between me and Calynn.

"My lady, I am going to do you a favor and pretend this didn't happen. You should change back into your normal clothes before anyone else sees you trying to impersonate the princess."

"But I am—"

He held up a hand, cutting me off. "Don't." He pulled his other hand out of my grasp.

I released the glamour from my eyes, letting them fade slowly from the silver that was Calynn's natural eye color to my entirely human blue. I wasn't exactly supposed to be using magic, though using glamour here didn't seem to be much of an issue. It was the only glamour I'd needed since I wore her clothes, stolen from her room, and other than our eyes, we were identical, a by-product of our connection as changelings who were switched with one another.

I frowned at Ronan. "I was careful. You shouldn't have been able to tell."

"And you shouldn't be trying to pass yourself off as the princess. What are you thinking?"

I couldn't say anything that wouldn't get me in trouble, so I just straightened my shoulders and said nothing.

Eventually, Ronan shook his head. "Be on your way. I must be on mine."

I watched his retreating back until he turned a corner and was gone. Then I went outside. He shouldn't have been able to tell I wasn't Calynn. My glamour had been perfect. Of course, there was the difference in our magics. But magic permeated everything in the Sidhe. It was impossible to separate what belonged to a person versus what belonged to the world unless you concentrated.

I wasn't paying particular attention to where I was going. I should have stopped to change. Anyone who saw me would question why I was wearing Calynn's clothes, especially since I didn't feel comfortable returning the glamour to my eyes. If Ronan could figure out I wasn't Calynn, who else might?

I wandered for a while, lost in my thoughts. When I came back to the present, I found myself just beyond the eastern border of Calynn's property. I was at the edge of a forested area and knew better than to enter it without knowing anything about it. I'm not made of magic like the fae, but I can use it. While I had more access to magic than the average human, I was certainly no match for some—a lot—of the creatures who lived here.

Then I heard a small cry.

I hesitated. Someone could be trying to trick me, to lure me out of a place of safety in order to attack. But the cry sounded like a wounded bird. My heart urged me to go, ensure the creature wasn't injured, while my head told me to stay. The forest was a dangerous place.

The cry came again, and I decided. I stepped into the forest, toward the sound, careful to keep the property behind me visible through the trees. It wasn't far when I found the little bird on the ground. It was from the finch family with a red breast, black head, and black wings. And it was a baby. It must have fallen out of the tree. I found the nest quickly, the cheeping of the fallen one's siblings guiding me. I crouched next to the baby.

"Well, hello, little one." I reached down and carefully scooped the baby into my hand. "You remind me of a friend of mine. He also tried to fly before he was ready. He got there eventually, though. You will, too."

I lifted him toward his nest above my head. He wiggled around and I got him into his home just as the mother returned with breakfast.

"Everyone is safe," I told the mother. She didn't pay me any attention as she disappeared into the nest. I turned back to the property and started toward the house. Now I had calmed a bit, I could figure out my next move.

I wanted to cause Calynn pain. After everything I had endured in her absence these last twenty-nine years, she deserved to feel a little of what I felt. And since she spent the majority of her time away from her Winter estate, I only had a few more hours to plot something new.

***

After changing out of Calynn's clothes and into a lovely blue day dress that matched my eyes, I made my way to the library. I paused outside the door, considering the character I needed to play. A woman, ruled by passion, intent on ensuring she can be with her lover against all odds.

I threw the door open and swept through, a look of terror on my face. I took half a second to appreciate the startled expressions of Calynn and her house manager Cacey as I paused, framed by the door.

"Ronan and I want to be together," I said, rushing the words out as though I couldn't keep them in any longer.

They stared at me for a long moment and then Cacey began gathering up some papers that had been spread on the desk.

"Perhaps I should leave you," he said.

Calynn nodded. "Come back in about an hour."

"Shall I fetch Ronan?"

"That shouldn't be necessary."

Cacey stood with the papers and gave Calynn a shallow bow before he left the room, barely acknowledging me as he moved past. I didn't let the annoyance show on my face, but I noted his disrespect.

Calynn pointed her pencil toward me. "Come in and close the door."

I did and flipped my hair over my shoulder as I sat in the chair Cacey had just vacated.

"Now. You want to run that by me again?"

She didn't look particularly concerned as she spun the pencil between both hands. Indignant anger rushed through me. Did she think I was so beneath her notice that nothing I did would harm her? Did she think me so unworthy of love that no one could possibly want me?

"We slept together this afternoon. He loves me and I love him and we want to be together."

She set the pencil down and leaned back in her chair, regarding me. She looked at me for so long that I fought not to fidget under her scrutiny. I reminded myself of the part I was playing: I was a woman who wanted a man, willing to do whatever it took to get what she wanted. I was desperate to be in the arms of my lover.

Finally, she leaned forward again. "Okay, let's pretend for a minute that I *can't* tell you're lying. We can also pretend Ronan didn't already tell me exactly what happened this afternoon. Do you know how difficult it is for a full fae to fall in love, not just have some love for a moment, but actually *fall in love* with a human? Setting aside our differences in magic, there's the lifespan to consider. Daoine sidhe live to be three thousand years old. You're going to live around three hundred years if you remain in the Sidhe. Now, I'm not saying it's impossible, especially given how long you've lived in the Sidhe, but it's extremely unlikely."

My mouth dropped open.

"You—he—how—"

The door opened again, and Ronan entered the library. He closed the door softly behind him and genuine terror flooded me when I noticed the violent anger in his eyes. It was quite possible I had taken this too far.

"I said it wouldn't be necessary to call you in," Calynn said as Ronan strode past me to stand next to her.

"If someone is telling lies about me, I deserve the chance to defend myself."

"You think I would ever believe what she said was true?" Calynn stood so the two of them were close together.

I maintained my composure, but inside, I called myself every kind of fool. They never showed their intimacy in public. I had thought he had feelings for her, but not that those feelings were reciprocated. It was as clear as glass—now they were in this private setting—I had severely misjudged their relationship.

"Have you been with anyone since you've been with me?" Calynn asked quietly. I could tell she asked for his benefit and not because she thought he had.

"I haven't been with anyone but you for the past six months."

"We've only known each other for three months."

"I know."

One of his hands traced her cheek and my frustration bubbled up as he leaned down and kissed her. It wasn't a long kiss, but I could see the affection they shared. They didn't even care that I was watching. In fact, I wondered if the show was partly *because* I was watching.

I crossed my arms over my chest and looked away. From the corner of my eye, I saw Calynn resume her seat and regard me. Ronan took up a spot right behind her.

I refused to acknowledge them.

"Come on, Nialas. Stop acting like a petulant child for not getting your way."

I glared back at her.

"You tried a move. You lost. Get over it. Obviously, you were trying to separate me from Ronan. I have a few guesses as to why. You want to enlighten me on which one is right?"

I thought furiously for a moment. What could I say that she might believe?

"I didn't know you were together. He's not a noble after all. And I find him beautiful. I just hoped to be with him. Even if he thought I was you."

"Try again."

"Excuse me?"

"The truth, Nialas. Or get the fuck out of my office."

My eyes widened before I could school my expression. How could she possibly know I was lying?

She sat back again, completely relaxed. Like nothing I did could possibly bother her. Like I was nothing of consequence.

"I'm told it's called glamour blind and is the reason fae changelings were outlawed. Whatever. I know when people are lying. I can even see through glamour. It's probably also why you're so *good* at it, given our connection. And lying, for that matter. But you can't lie to me."

I stared. I couldn't think. How could I accomplish anything if I couldn't lie or hide behind my glamour? How did she know I had glamour? It was forbidden for humans to use magic in the Sidhe. While I'd noticed a lack of punishment for my own use of it here, I had thought it was because no one had been paying attention.

"Look," she said, spreading her hands in an open gesture. "It's just us. I won't punish you for whatever you say. I swear. Tell me the truth."

I glanced at Ronan and noted Calynn's "just us" included him. They were more intimate than I could have ever imagined. I wondered how close they actually were and if it was something I could use. For now, she had sworn she wouldn't punish me for whatever I said. It was my chance to say some things I'd always wanted to say.

"I hate you," I said, and I didn't fight to contain the loathing dripping from my voice. "I hate how you have everything I ever wanted and you don't care about any of it. I hate how you have the loyalty of your friends, yet no one even looks at me. I'm invisible here, even though I look exactly like you. Even though I am your sister in everything but blood. My whole life you have been set up as a paragon which I could never live up to. You represent everything I despise about the Sidhe. And I wanted to hurt you."

As I spoke, I watched as Calynn began to smile. The smile continued to grow the more I talked, and it caused the rage to grow within me. She couldn't even take my declaration seriously. But when I finished, I noticed her hand had come out in a gesture to stop Ronan from drawing his sword. He took me seriously. The fiery anger in his eyes matched the anger in me and I was nervous he might ignore Calynn's gesture and cut me down where I sat.

"Your honesty is refreshing, *sister*. In exchange, let me offer my own. I don't hate you, Nialas. I pity you. Not for any of the reasons you just stated, but because you let your anger rule you instead of seeing what's right in front of you."

"And what is that?"

She shrugged. "Could be a lot of things. From me? I want to give you an opportunity, but you probably won't accept it."

Whatever opportunity she could offer me, I was certain I didn't want it. I didn't need her handouts or leftovers. I sat silently, not willing to entertain the unspoken offer.

She twitched her head in a gesture toward the door. "Go. We're done for now. You don't want to hear anything more from me, anyway."

I stood with all the regal bearing I could call to me, chin lifted, shoulders back, and swept toward the door. Before I could open it, Calynn called out.

"Oh. One more thing, Nialas." She stood and came around her desk to stand next to me, moving with a steady confidence that needed no augmentation of style. "The people here are under my protection. All of them. You will not attempt to seduce anyone who is unwilling again. You may express interest, and if it is not reciprocated, you will *back off*. Immediately. In addition, you will not use anyone who is under my protection to try to exact some childish idea of revenge against me. Do I make myself clear?"

I'd lived my entire life among predators, people who could kill me with little more than a thought. Calynn had never struck me as dangerous before—so much smaller than everyone else, so much more laid back—until this moment.

"I understand."

Her inhuman silver eyes searched me for a long time, and I actually felt a sense of relief that she could hear lies because she would be certain I told the truth.

Then the fierce look faded, and she sighed.

"I don't want us to be enemies. I've got enough of those. I brought you here for a reason. Maybe we can never be friends, but hopefully we can find a way to co-exist?"

I was about to say of course we could, but she would be able to hear the lie. Instead, I went against my nature and told her the truth. "I don't know."

Chapter 2

I tossed and turned all night, finally waking up early, more tired than when I'd gone to bed. Calynn's words had plagued my dreams.

I want to give you an opportunity, but you probably won't accept it.

I brought you here for a reason.

What possible reason could she have to bring me here other than to make me miserable? I dressed myself, my anger still simmering. When I'd lived with Mother and Father, I'd had maids who helped me dress each morning and styled my hair. I'd had a vast wardrobe and so much jewelry that I could never decide what to wear.

Here, I had nothing. No maids, no jewelry, only a few simple dresses. I'd had to leave Glacia quickly, moving from Father's dungeons directly to Calynn's estate. I hadn't had any time to pack anything.

What kind of opportunity would require Calynn to bring me here with nothing? She obviously wanted me dependent on her.

I left my room, the smallest room available. Her *maid* had a larger room than I. How could she possibly think I would want an opportunity from her? It probably came with strings attached, just like everything else the fae ever gave.

In the kitchen, Calynn's cook had made fresh muffins.

"Good morning, Lady Nialas," the cook said as I came in. "Your treats for the horses are there."

I found the bowl of apple slices and carrot chunks and took a muffin, still steaming. Daric had been getting the treats for the horses ready for me every day before I arrived in the kitchen. It had started almost immediately after I arrived, a consideration I was certain Calynn had encouraged. But I would not be grateful for someone trying to manipulate me into it.

I made my way out to the stables where Bainbridge, Calynn's stable master, was already cleaning the stalls, the horses turned out into the paddock. He was half daoine sidhe and half selkie, an odd combination. We nodded to each other as the horses noticed me and sauntered over, snuffling at me.

I laughed, my anger fading. "All right, all right."

I gave each horse an apple slice and a carrot chunk, stroking their long noses as they chewed. After they were done, they checked me to be sure I was completely out of food and then moved off to eat some grass. I watched them go with a smile. I was about to leave when Bainbridge stopped me.

"Good morning, Lady Nialas," he said, exiting the paddock. "Are you off on your morning walk?"

"I am."

"You'll want to avoid the eastern fields today. The twins have done something, and the snow has melted, creating a fair amount of mud."

I set off, my ire raising again. Another person Calynn had probably instructed to be kind to me. I wouldn't fall for their tricks.

I liked to walk in the morning when the birds were out finding their breakfast. They swooped through the skies, catching bugs, or pecked at the ground. I noted a few, but they were too far for me to figure out what kind of birds they were.

I passed the two mongrel siblings who worked in Calynn's fields, and they each gave me a nod and said good morning. My walk complete, I returned inside and sat in the solarium, where I liked to read before lunch.

The two young brownies, the housekeeper's and cook's children, were playing a game on the floor. They looked up at me with a smile.

"Good morning, Lady Nialas," they said together, before continuing on with their game.

I sat in the seat I'd been using and picked up the book, my mind drifting as I tried to read, Calynn's words from yesterday still pestering me.

You let your anger rule you instead of seeing what's right in front of you.

It wasn't true. All that was in front of me was a quiet, boring life of visiting horses and reading books. Before Calynn stole me from Glacia, I had parties to attend. People envied me.

Yes, Father had put me into the dungeon, but I was certain he would have let me out eventually if Calynn hadn't taken me away.

...what's right in front of you.

I looked up from my book to the brownies, who were currently right in front of me. What could I be missing? There was nothing. I had *nothing*. No friends, no occupation, no possessions.

I tried to read again, but her words distracted me. If she brought me here for a reason, if she had an opportunity for me, what harm could there be in hearing her out? Whatever the reason, I probably wouldn't want to have anything to do with it. But if it was something interesting, I could use her to gain something I wanted. I stood, suddenly certain I had to figure this out immediately.

The young brownies paused their game. "Good day, Lady Nialas," they said together.

I paused as I considered them, brownie children playing a game. How could anyone be that happy in this world?

***

Quinn—Calynn's maid who used to be mine—told me her mistress was in the library, so I went there only to find a guard posted at the door, which was unusual. He was taller than me, though that wasn't difficult. He stood with the same air and confidence all guards stood with. And just like all of them, he was fit and gorgeous. Dark hair, long enough to slide fingers through, fell in soft waves over his forehead. Broad shoulders that looked strong enough to hold the world.

I shook myself from my wayward thoughts, reaching for the doorknob, but he stopped me.

"The princess asked not to be disturbed."

His eyes found mine and I was struck by the very human, warm brown color of them. He was a mongrel—half daoine sidhe, half human. His kind were typically disdained in the Sidhe. Yet here he was, guarding my sister like he was as important as any of them.

"Don't be ridiculous," I said. "I'm her sister. She can't have meant me."

"She meant everyone. She gave explicit instructions that no one is to open the door until she does."

"It's the library. What if I want to read a book?"

"Then you will wait until the princess opens the door."

I stared at him a moment, my hand still on the knob, his hand like a warm band around my wrist. I considered whether I would be able to get past him if I moved fast enough. He didn't seem to think I would try, as he held me lightly. I could use that to my advantage.

"Fine," I said. "I'll return later."

He lifted his hand, and as soon as he did, I turned the knob and pushed the door open. The mongrel tried to stop me, but it was too late. The door was open, revealing Calynn with her back to me, sitting on the desk with Ronan between her knees. They had been kissing deeply, but stopped when I stepped in.

"Princess!" the mongrel said, looking alarmed. "I tried to stop her. I didn't think she would actually—"

Calynn slid off the desk with a sigh, her body brushing against Ronan's before she moved around him.

"It's fine, Andras. Nialas is proving difficult to anticipate."

She stopped in front of me, leaning against the desk.

"Back to your post," Ronan said. He hadn't moved since I came in.

The mongrel returned to the other side of the door and closed it behind him.

Calynn crossed her arms over her chest. "Well? You came in here for a reason."

I gave myself an internal shake and lifted my chin. "You said you brought me here for something. I would know what that reason is."

"Would you?" She considered me for a long moment before she continued. "You owe a debt, Nialas. I brought you here so you could repay it."

"A debt for what?" Despite my intention to hear her out before dismissing her, I heard the sneer in my voice, but I couldn't stop it. "I am not fae. I am not beholden to the same laws you are."

Calynn stared at me, her silver gaze peering deep into me. Far deeper than I felt comfortable. I held myself rigid, refusing to squirm under her inspection.

"You're right, of course. You aren't required to pay the debt. I'll have someone take you to the human world tomorrow. That should give you enough time to pack."

I felt like someone had doused me with icy water. "Excuse me?"

She shrugged one shoulder. "If you don't want to pay the debt because you're human, you're free to live in the human world." She stood straight, uncrossing her arms to point at me, all trace of indifference gone from her bearing, anger simmering in those inhuman eyes. "Just because some of the daoine sidhe have decided the only debts they'll enforce are the ones that benefit them, doesn't mean I'm going to be the same. I won't cause the imbalance to get worse and I'm not going to allow you to make it worse, either. If you want to remain in this world among the fae, you will follow the laws of the fae. You can't have it both ways, Nialas."

She moved around her desk to sit down again.

"Listen. If you want to go to the human world and start a new life there, you're welcome to take over the life of Calynn D'Arcy. You can even have the name since it seemed so important to you before. I don't have much, but it's all yours if you want it. There's a few thousand dollars, some furniture, a business that has pretty much failed. I doubt you'd want to be a private investigator, anyway. You can't have my bike. Otherwise, you can have everything."

I considered the idea. A new life. Start over among people who were like me. Humans. There must be something I could do. I wouldn't have to speak to any of the people here who had always teased me, ignored me, or worse. But if I left the Sidhe, I might lose all access to magic. I couldn't lose my magic. It was the only thing that made me special, even if I did have to keep it secret. And I didn't want to lose my access to the magical creatures in the Sidhe either. Some of them were fascinating, and I wanted to study them more.

"I want to stay," I said.

Calynn tapped her fingers against the desk, considering me. "All right. Then what do you propose?"

"I don't know. What is the debt for and what would you have me do to repay it?"

"The debt is for your role in Meriel's death."

"The selkie?" I hadn't thought anyone cared. No one seemed to care about the fate of exiled fae.

"Yes. And as for what you can do, what are you good at?"

Choosing the appropriate dress for the occasion, blending in with a crowd, being who the person I'm with wanted me to be. None of those were things Calynn would find useful. Unless...

"I could return to Glacia," I offered. "You have many enemies there and I have the freedom to watch them. I could send reports back to you on their movements."

"Spy for me?" she asked.

"It would be useful to know if the Queen was planning something," Ronan said.

My eyes shot to him. He'd been so still, I'd almost forgotten he was there.

"I agree. But it's not what I expected you to say," Calynn said, still watching me carefully. After a moment, her eyes flashed with disappointment, though I couldn't understand why. "All right. Return to Glacia. See what you can find. Report back. If it doesn't work out, we'll try something else."

I left the library to pack. This would work out. Because I had a new plan and if I played it right, I could repay my "debt" and hurt Calynn at the same time.

CHAPTER 3

Before I could leave, someone knocked on my bedroom door. I opened it to find Calynn on the other side with the mongrel who had tried to stop me from entering the library.

"What is it?" I asked, looking from one to the other.

"It occurred to me," Calynn said, "returning to Glacia, after I took you from Queran's estate, might make things dangerous for you. I'm sending a guard with you."

I glanced at the mongrel again. While she might have a point, I refused to concede that to her. "A babysitter, you mean."

"If that's how you want to look at it." She gestured to the mongrel. "Nialas, this is Andras. He is loyal to me." She paused, her silver gaze hard, and I understood the warning.

I nodded.

"He'll make sure you're safe. Good luck in Glacia."

She walked away, leaving me alone with the mongrel.

"Whenever you're ready to leave," he said.

"Don't you need to pack anything?"

"You don't need to worry about me, Lady Nialas."

I went back into my room and finished with the last of my items. I didn't have much. It would be nice to return to Glacia for a while, even if only to gather the few items I actually cared about.

The mongrel and I left shortly after. We took a couple of horses and made our way through the forest paths back to the city. Considering the date, Father might not even be there. He usually went to our estate near the Summer border at this time of year to be with Mother. I should be with him. But it would be better not to have to see him after everything around the Winter Solstice. I'd definitely screwed that one up. I should never have challenged Calynn to a duel. I'd wanted to prove to the Queen that she could count on me, but I'd neglected to factor in what my father would do when he found out. As it was, he'd stopped the duel and locked me in a dungeon. Since I hadn't actually killed Calynn, I was certain he would have let me out, eventually.

My new plan would be much better. I spent the ride considering all the things I would have to do to undermine Calynn's influence in the city. She'd made a few friends while she was there over the Winter Solstice, and impressed everyone when she'd taken part in the challenges. She'd completed every one of the elemental challenges—fire, earth, water, air, metal, light, flora, and darkness—to the third and final task. This was completely unheard of before. Of course, I'd been in the dungeon by that point.

There must be something I could do. Though it was going to be more difficult to accomplish anything with a shadow who was loyal to Calynn.

"Why did she send you with me, anyway?" I asked him. "It's not like I will need protection in the city."

"Of course not, my lady," he said dryly. "You just look exactly like the woman who the queens are both trying to kill. Even if they don't mistake you for her, they also know she took you from Prince Queran's dungeons, so you're obviously important to her. You may not believe you're in danger by going back to the city, but you will not exactly be safe, either."

The idea of being in danger in the only home I'd ever known made my palms sweat, but I scoffed, disguising the fear with a look of disdain.

"What do you know? You're just a mongrel."

He snorted. "That's rich, coming from you."

I wheeled toward him. "Are you implying I am as low as a mongrel?"

"No. I'm implying you're lower. At least to them. Do you think they hate me just because I'm a half-breed? If that was the case, they'd hate Bainbridge too, but they don't. Even though he's not fully daoine sidhe, he *is* fully fae. I'm half human. It's the human half they can't stand."

I gaped at him. No one had ever dared speak to me in that manner. Everyone had always feared my father's wrath if someone treated me poorly. Father's pride demanded he protect what was his, and he did so with ferocity.

"Oh," the mongrel continued before I could respond, "and Princess Calynn has forbidden the term mongrel. If you know what's good for you, you won't use it around her or her people." He shrugged. "I suppose there's nothing I can do about it while we're away. But when she's around, I wouldn't push my luck."

I turned resolutely around, my back as straight as I could make it, and refused to respond. I knew everything he said was true. Calynn had already mentioned to me about the term "mongrel," but what else were you supposed to call them? And I had lived in the Sidhe my entire life, minus the first month or so. I knew exactly what the daoine sidhe and the rest of the fae thought of humans. It was why I spent so much energy appearing to be exactly what other people wanted me to be.

"Are you nervous about going back?" the mongrel asked.

"Nervous about what?"

"Well, the last time you were in Glacia, your father threw you in a dungeon."

"He was just annoyed. I'm sure he's over it by now."

"Right. I'm sure everyone who annoys someone gets thrown into dungeons. If the princess hadn't rescued you, you'd probably still be there."

"Calynn stole me from my home and is now claiming I owe her a debt. You think that's better than getting to stay in the home I've always known?"

He lifted one eyebrow at me. "You have a funny way of seeing things, Lady Nialas."

His statement sounded so much like what Calynn had told me, I again twisted in the saddle to look at him. "What do you mean by that?"

"You say she stole you from the only home you knew. But did you like it there?"

"Of course I liked it there. It's my home."

"My mother's house was my home for the first fifteen years of my life. I never liked it there."

It was on the tip of my tongue to ask what happened after those first fifteen years—where had his home been then—but I didn't want to seem interested in him. He was a mongrel. People of my social standing didn't associate with mongrels. Even if the mongrel in question had beautiful brown eyes with golden flecks that seemed to see right into my soul.

I turned away without acknowledging his words and stared straight ahead. I didn't even look around when he chuckled at my obvious dismissal, even though I wanted to.

When we reached Glacia and my father's home, a butler stopped me as we entered and requested I follow him. The mongrel trailed behind without speaking, and the butler led me to my father's office.

He was sitting at his desk, going over some paperwork.

"What are you doing here?" he asked without looking up at me.

"Calynn allowed me to return," I said, not sure what I should say next. Since I was supposed to be spying for her, I figured I shouldn't say too much.

In the end, it didn't matter.

"Regardless of what she has allowed, you are no longer welcome here," Father said.

"I am no longer welcome in my home?"

He finally looked up at me with such hatred that I took a step back. "You think I would take in someone who tried to murder my daughter?"

I couldn't breathe.

"But, Father... *I'm* your daughter."

"Not anymore."

The cold finality in his voice cut me, slicing into wounds as old as I was. I'd known my whole life he and my mother loved Calynn more than me. They'd wanted her back from the very moment they'd sent her away. I'd always thought they cared about me as well, in their own way. Now, I wondered if it had ever been true.

"You may go to your room and pack anything you wish to take with you," he said, looking back at his papers, effectively dismissing me. "Then I am quit of you. I want you gone within the hour."

I stood motionless in the doorway for a few seconds. For eternity. Then the mongrel touched my shoulder.

I turned to him and his brown gaze locked onto mine. I found the strength to move away from my father's office and led us to my bedroom.

.

Chapter 4

I left the door to my suite open so he could come in or not on his own. Then I sat on the couch in my sitting area, determined not to cry, my eyes burning as I stared into the empty hearth. A few tears managed to escape my rigid hold, tracing down my cheeks.

The mongrel followed me in, and I tracked his blurry movements as he came closer to me, waiting for him to make some snide remark. Instead, he handed me a handkerchief. He didn't strike me as the type to carry one. Yet the plain white cloth with an embroidered border hovered in front of my face and I took it gently from his hand.

"I know what it feels like to not be wanted," he said. "It's not a feeling I would wish on anyone."

I ran my fingers along the embroidered lines on the edge of the fabric, one blue, one purple. I peered up into his human eyes, as if seeing him for the first time. He didn't regard me with pity or rancor, though I'd certainly given him ample reason to do so. Instead, he looked at me with a simple understanding I'd never seen in someone before.

"What do you want to do now?" he asked.

"I don't know what I can do," I said, using the cloth to wipe away my tears. "I have nowhere to go. My father has cast me out. I have no way to repay the debt Calynn claims I owe. I..." I stared off into the distance and Andras settled next to me.

"You can return to her estate. She won't turn you away."

"You know her so well?"

"I pay attention. She won't turn anyone away who needs her. She is what the daoine sidhe are meant to be."

I wondered if he had feelings for her. It was the only reason I could think of for him to speak of his leader in such a kind way. Especially someone like him who had probably only known cruelty from the people who were supposed to protect him.

"All right," I said, deciding to trust him. "Let us return to my sister so I may throw myself on her mercy."

He flashed me a grin and then stood. "What are you going to pack?"

We spent some time going through the things in my room. I admitted there were few pieces of jewelry I actually cared about and only took a single necklace—a scarlet scale on a simple chain. I found a few dresses I didn't want to leave behind and packed them with my necklace in a trunk.

I went to my bookcase next.

"I want to take them all," I said, trailing my fingers over the spines, lingering on special ones.

"There isn't enough space in the trunk for them all, but I'm sure the princess can retrieve the ones left behind."

I nodded and pulled a slim book off the shelf. *Tales on the Wing* written by Keilah. It was my favorite out of all my books. I found a few more and packed them with the dresses.

Finally, I went into my bedroom and picked up the small white bear I had on my bedside table. I couldn't remember a time in my life when I hadn't had Baby Brother Ted and, even though he'd probably been Calynn's before mine, I couldn't leave him behind. I placed him on top of the dresses in the trunk and then closed it, latching the buckle.

"That's all?" Andras asked. "There's so many things left in here. There's space for a few more books."

I cast a look around the room, my gaze lighting on one thing after another I had previously thought so important. "Save the books, none of these things feel like mine," I said.

"Why didn't you bring these with you before?" he asked, pointing to the trunk.

"You know I challenged Calynn to a duel," I said, moving to sit on the couch again.

Andras took a seat on the far corner, turning toward me. "I did."

"I almost won, though I doubt I'd be able to if I tried again. She seemed distracted that night. My father..." I stumbled over the word, fresh tears coming to my eyes. I wiped them away with the handkerchief I still held. "Prince Queran stopped me and threw me in the dungeon. Calynn got me out a few days later and sent me directly to her estate. I didn't have a chance to come back here. And I didn't want to ask her for anything."

"That was rather self-destructive."

"How do you figure?"

"You could have just asked her for help, but you let your pride get in your way."

I opened my mouth to refute his statement, but I found I couldn't. He was absolutely right. Calynn's own words came back to me again. *You let your anger rule you instead of seeing what's right in front of you.* I'd been so angry, I'd let it prevent me from simply asking to pack a few things before I left Glacia. Or even to ask if I could return for the things later.

"Will we be able to get the trunk back? We only have the two horses."

"I'm sure we can rent a cart," he said.

I stood and handed him back the handkerchief.

He shook his head. "Keep it. Consider it a gift, freely given."

I stared at him, but he had already moved on, checking to ensure the trunk was securely fastened. As though he gave gifts all the time. As though the kindness was something he offered to people every day. I'd only ever received one other gift, the necklace already packed in my trunk. I carefully folded the fabric, with its simple embroidery, and tucked it away in my pocket.

We left Glacia only a few hours after we arrived, a cart hooked up to Andras' horse loaded with my single trunk.

We made slow progress through the forest, and I was grateful for the extra time. I was in no hurry to return to Calynn and tell her of my complete failure. The winter sun shone through the trees, creating a beautiful afternoon.

"Isn't the sun so..." I said when a shadow crossed over us, blocking the very light I had been about to praise.

We stopped and Andras drew a sword from his side with a hiss of metal. He kept a close eye on the sky, so when the shape dove out of it, he was ready to intercept it. That didn't stop the scarlet legs from knocking Andras to the ground, his horse jerking in the opposite direction with a frightened whinny. Despite the fall, Andras struck the attacking creature before it flew up into the sky again. It spun in a graceful arc before streaking back to the fallen man, pinning his sword arm to the ground.

The wyvern released a loud screech and poised his tail to sting with his poisonous barb.

"Derecho, don't!" I screamed. "He's my friend."

The whole interaction had only taken a few seconds. When Derecho heard my voice, he immediately lifted himself into the sky out of Andras' reach and flew over to me, chattering wildly.

"Calm down," I said. "I can't understand you when you talk that fast."

He perched on a tree branch near my head, and it dipped under his weight. He spread his wings wide for balance, showing off the long finger-like bones connecting the leathery skin that allowed him to fly. Once the branch settled, he folded his wings behind him. He had grown since the last time I'd seen him, now the size of a large eagle, though much heavier.

He snapped his beak together in frustration.

"Now. Tell me what you came to say," I said.

He chirped and clicked.

Andras had recovered himself and his horse. I felt him staring at me and my wyvern friend.

"Merciful Mother," he whispered, his voice laced with awe.

I barely noticed as Derecho explained why he had found me. A chill swept through my body as I listened to the story. When he finished, I turned to Andras.

"We must get back to Calynn. Now."

He stared at me for only a second before he climbed back on the horse. We started toward Calynn's estate quicker than before, urging the horses into a canter. I wanted to go faster, but Andras' horse couldn't gallop while pulling the cart.

When we had settled into a steady pace, Andras asked, "What's wrong?"

"Derecho's aerie was attacked. His family is in danger."

CHAPTER 5

Calynn had already left her estate by the time we returned. I paced the library while I waited for someone to bring her from wherever she stayed when she wasn't here. Derecho perched on one of the chairs while Andras stood just inside the door, watching me pace.

Derecho let out a screech.

"I know," I told him. "But I can't go anywhere without telling her." I grimaced, hating the fact she had been right before: if I wanted to remain in the Sidhe, I had to follow the laws of the Sidhe. "I owe a debt and she holds it."

Derecho chittered in sympathy. I smiled at him and stopped for a moment to stroke the scarlet scales on his head, avoiding the horns finally beginning to grow in.

Outside the library, someone shouted and footsteps came closer and closer until the door opened and Calynn entered, Ronan trailing just behind her.

"There's an emergency?" she asked, her eyes catching on Derecho before she moved to sit behind her desk.

"Derecho's aerie was attacked yesterday. I need to help him."

She looked at Derecho again. "Tell me what happened." I started to answer, but she held up her hand. "I'd like to hear it from him."

I blinked a few times. Not many people could understand a wyvern. It had taken me a full year to learn the difference between his chirps and screeches. Another year after that for the sounds to make sense as a form of communication. But as Derecho recounted the attack on his aerie, Calynn nodded as though she understood everything. She even asked questions occasionally during his story.

He told her about how he'd been hunting while his sister remained at the nest brooding her eggs. She'd laid seven last month.

"How long before they're ready to hatch?" Calynn asked.

Another five months. And his sister couldn't leave them for longer than a few hours or else they would get too cold and die. So Derecho, with his sister's mate, had been doing all the hunting for her. She was only a hundred years old. This was her first brood, and she was terribly nervous.

"Any first-time parent would be. So you and her mate were both out hunting?"

And when Derecho returned, something had attacked the aerie. His sister had been rendered unconscious and one of the eggs stolen. Now she wants her mate to remain at the nest for added protection and she hoped the White Hart could help her move her brood to keep them safe from further attack. Derecho didn't know how to find the Stag, so he'd come to find Nialas instead, since Nialas researched so much about the creatures living in the Sidhe.

"Why does your sister think there will be further attacks?"

Derecho chittered his response. Their mother's aerie had been close to where his sister's aerie was. It had been attacked many times. It was the hunting ground of some creature who stole eggs from the nests. Derecho's own egg had been one such, but Nialas had rescued him and raised him until he could find his family.

"Why did your sister—nevermind. It's not important. My fear is, even if we move your sister's brood, there are many creatures in the Sidhe who would attack a nest and steal the eggs."

This creature is different. It does more than just steal eggs. It sometimes kills the wyverns who live there. Kills them but does not eat them. It only ever takes the eggs. His sister hoped the creature had left the area when she built her aerie. She was mistaken, and now her nest is at risk.

Calynn regarded Derecho, tapping her fingers on the desk in front of her.

"It's odd the creature kills the wyvern but only takes the eggs. Still, you know the Stag can't interfere in situations between a predator and its prey."

"That's not fair," I exclaimed.

Calynn's regard switched to me. "How is it not? If I interfere between a predator and its prey, the predator starves. I won't upset the balance in this realm further by involving myself in something I shouldn't. The Sidhe has already swung too far out of balance because of people acting against their nature."

I began to argue and then my jaw snapped shut as I realized what she'd just said. "What do you mean, *you* won't involve yourself? I thought we were talking about the White Hart."

She motioned to the antler necklace I'd seen her wearing lately. She never seemed to take it off. "I'm the Stag's champion. We met a few weeks back, and he gave me a little more responsibility." Her mouth twisted into something that was neither a grimace nor a smile, but somewhere in between. "How do you think I understand what Derecho's saying? It's not like I've met another wyvern before."

"If you won't do something, I will," I said as I turned to the door.

"Sit down, Nialas. We'll figure something out, but we're not going to do anything without thinking things through first." Ronan made a funny noise and Calynn didn't look at him when she said, "Don't start."

"Of course not, my princess."

She tapped her fingers against the desk again. "I can help move the nest," she said. "I can't guarantee it'll be a safer place unless the nest is brought here. I can't do anything about the creature unless it begins breaking the laws."

"How might it break the laws?" I asked.

"If it kills for the sake of it and not for food. If it harms someone for the sake of it. If it takes more than it can reasonably use. We can't be certain this creature is the same one from when Derecho's mother lived there. So far, it hasn't done anything other than hurt his sister to take the egg. It's possible the creature took the egg to eat it."

Derecho chirped again, and Calynn turned back to him with a smile. "You and your family are welcome here. I'll be glad to help where I can." She sighed, her smile slipping. "Though I am fucking busy at the moment. Being pulled in a million directions at once." She returned her attention to me. "Were you serious about helping Derecho?"

"Of course."

She tapped her fingers again. "You still owe a debt. Help Derecho move his nest to this property and I'll consider your debt repaid. I'll send someone to help you." She looked past me to where Andras still stood at the door. "Are you willing?"

"I am, Princess."

She rolled her eyes. "I'm certain I told you not to call me that." She turned to Ronan. "Your thoughts?"

"Andras is competent. If the task is just to move the nest, he will be sufficient to protect Lady Nialas and the nest. Especially if the mother and father accompany them. And Derecho. If they are to take on a creature, I would want to know what kind of creature. But something that feels comfortable attacking a hundred-year-old wyvern?" He shook his head. "I would suggest at least another five people. Probably more."

"The idea isn't to attack the creature. Just move the nest. If they can make it here, I'll be able to keep them safe. No one hunts on my land." She looked directly at Derecho. "That includes you. When you hunt, you'll leave the property. Everyone here is under my protection."

Derecho chirped the affirmative. Calynn nodded. "Fine. I'll figure out a good place for the new aerie while you're gone. In the meantime, I'm sending Nialas and Andras to help you move the nest to the property. I'd like a moment with Nialas."

Derecho was the first to move. He hopped off the chair and walked awkwardly to the door, his wings held above him for balance. Andras and Ronan followed him out.

"I know you want to help your friend as much as you can. Do not take this creature on under some desire to protect Derecho. If you interfere while working in the name of the White Hart, being human won't protect you from the repercussions."

"And if the creature breaks one of the laws?"

"Then its life is forfeit, and I will destroy it."

There it was again. To just look at her, a person could be forgiven for not fearing her. But in her eyes was a fierce protective fire telling me not to cross her. I had no doubt she could take on any creature and survive.

CHAPTER 6

I went to my room to pack for the trip and pulled my special things out of the trunk Andras and I had brought back to the estate. I set my necklace in a locking drawer and put Baby Brother Ted on the table next to my bed.

I gathered a few sets of clothes I usually reserved for working in the garden with Mother and had just changed into one when someone knocked on my bedroom door. I opened it, surprised to find Ronan standing on the other side. What reason could he possibly have to be here? Maybe Calynn had changed her mind about helping Derecho. I couldn't let her do that.

"I would like a word before you leave," he said, not stepping past my threshold.

Andras stood outside the door and I cast a glance at him. He looked just as confused by the marshal's presence as I was.

"Of course," I said, moving aside so Ronan could enter my room. He left the door open behind him.

"I've been thinking a lot about what you said when you told Calynn you hated her."

I heard Andras' startled noise outside, but I ignored him, focusing instead on Ronan as he moved around my room, almost pacing.

"Your hatred is misplaced," he declared.

"I can hate whomever I want for whatever reason I want."

"I am not saying otherwise. But I'd like to correct one of your mistaken beliefs so you can see if the hatred is warranted." He stopped his not-quite-pacing and turned to me. "Calynn is not responsible for what's happened to you. I am."

My mouth dropped open, and I stared at Ronan in shock.

"You know you and Calynn were changed as infants. You know it was done under Prince Queran's orders. What you may not know is I am the one who decided to change her with *you*."

"You?"

"Yes. The Prince had to keep his orders somewhat vague so the Queen couldn't punish him for creating a fae changeling. I offered to take full responsibility so any punishment would fall to me alone. I spent a week in the human world looking for the right child. You had to be the same age, born on the same day, the right background. I couldn't very well place her with a Greek family or a Chinese family. It had to be a family who had roots in the old country but who didn't live in the old country because that's the first place the Queens would look for her. I still wanted her to be in a place where other fae might go, since the only type of person Calynn could ever be friends with would be a mongrel. I chose Vancouver. Three children matched all the requirements. Of the three, I chose you."

"Why me?"

His eyes lost focus for a moment. "At the time, it felt right." He focused again. "In the middle of the night, while your parents slept, I slipped into your bedroom and took you from your cradle. I brought you into the Sidhe and left Calynn in your place."

He said it without emotion. Cold facts about the abduction of an infant. That the infant had been me made no difference to him. There was no remorse or regret in his voice or his bearing.

"I would do it again," he said, confirming my thoughts. "A million times over. So if you must feel anger toward anyone for your life, it shouldn't be Calynn. She had no more choice in these matters than you did. I am the rightful owner of that anger."

"You just want to divert my hate away from Calynn," I said, uncertainty coloring my tone.

"That's not untrue. Neither is what I said." He paused, staring at something behind me. I turned to see he had noticed Baby Brother Ted sitting on my bedside table. The little white bear, ragged with age. He moved toward it slowly and picked it up.

I wanted to scream at him not to touch it, but that would be irrational. It was just a bear, after all. Instead, feigning indifference, I said, "It's probably just another thing that used to belong to Calynn."

"No. It's yours. He used to have a red shirt. I brought it with you when I brought you here." He turned, the bear in his hands. Baby Brother Ted seemed impossibly small in his grasp. "I knew what I was doing. I knew what kind of life I was setting you in. I didn't want you to be alone any more than I wanted Calynn to be alone. And I know what kind of life she lived out there, so I know what kind of life you lived in here. Something you may have overlooked in your anger, the magic in the Sidhe must have balance. However, a fae changeling is treated in the human world, so must the human changeling be treated in the fae world. What you felt, she felt."

I hadn't considered it like that before. All I had seen was how Mother and Father only cared about me when I could pose as a symbol of how their daughter had been changed against the Queens' wishes. Privately, they wanted the child they had lost. My human parents would have reacted the same way to Calynn, except she wouldn't have understood why.

"I will leave you to finish your packing. Good luck on your quest." He handed me Baby Brother Ted. "If you give him to one of the brownies, I'm certain they can restore him to his former self."

I clutched the small bear as Ronan left my room, stopping for a moment to speak to Andras before continuing away. I stared down at the stuffed toy. The only thing I kept from my childhood. I'd always wondered why this thing had meant more to me than any of the other, fancier things I had been given to play with. Things that had certainly meant to be for Calynn.

Ronan had brought me to this world with a bear. He didn't say he had brought anything with Calynn. What had she had to cling to as a small child in a world where no one wanted her around? I set Baby Brother Ted in his spot on my bedside table and returned to packing.

***

Just before we left, I removed the necklace from the drawer and put it on. The scarlet scale had belonged to Derecho, given as a gift before he left me to find his family five years ago. I'd only seen him a handful of times over the years since. They had been lonely ones.

Andras and I set out on foot. Derecho said some terrain would be difficult for horses and we didn't want to leave them unattended, possible prey for some creature. We walked in silence away from Calynn's estate, Derecho flying ahead of us. He stopped occasionally in a tree to wait for our much slower progress. I wanted to run, but I knew we had a long way to go and it would be unwise to use all our energy on the first day.

"Do you know where we're going?" Andras asked, suddenly.

We hadn't been able to figure out exactly where Derecho's nest was since he couldn't read a map. All he'd been able to tell us was that it was to the north, and it took him about a day to make the journey.

"No. But Derecho does."

I noticed Andras' jaw tighten, but he didn't say anything.

We continued on in silence until Andras stopped and glanced around. "This looks like a good place to stop for the night."

The weak winter sun still shone brightly in the sky. "We can keep going," I said.

"No. We need to set up camp."

He set his pack down and began removing items from it. I glared at him, but he didn't seem to notice.

"You set up camp if you want, but I'm going to keep on."

I turned and stalked away until an iron grip took hold of my arm, stopping me.

I glanced at the hand and then up at the man who held me.

"Lady Nialas," he began, but stopped when Derecho screeched and launched himself at Andras.

He stumbled backward, still holding my arm, and I fell with him. My weight threw Andras off balance, and we all landed on the ground in a tangle of limbs and wings. Derecho squawked indignantly as he struggled from the heap and took to the air again, leaving Andras and me to sort ourselves out. It was awkward as I tried to straighten, but ended up with my body flush against his, the scent of cedar enveloping me. His hands were still on my arms and my skin burned where he touched me. I gasped, rolling off him and sitting up.

Yet, I tingled everywhere. I ignored the feeling and stood, dusting myself off, hoping my face wasn't as red as it felt.

"I'm continuing on," I announced, turning my back on him. "Follow or don't. I don't care."

"Lady Nialas, wait."

I ignored him. I heard him scrambling after me, but didn't look. He eventually ran around me, holding his arms out to prevent me moving forward. Apparently, Derecho was only concerned if Andras grabbed me and not if he just stopped me, because he didn't interfere again.

"Get out of my way," I said.

"You're right that there is still daylight," he said. "However, darkness descends quickly, especially this time of year. We must set up camp now or else we will have to do it after nightfall."

Derecho perched in a tree above us, watching Andras carefully. He chittered a response.

"Derecho says twilight is still an hour away."

"Yes, Lady. But Derecho doesn't need to collect wood for a fire or set up a place to sleep. He can simply perch in a tree. We need to set out our bedrolls and put up a tent. Unless you want to sleep in the open."

I shuddered at the idea of sleeping in the open, on the frozen snow, where any creature might stumble across us. Even a tent offered little in the way of protection. I hesitated. I didn't want fear to stand in the way of getting me closer to helping Derecho, but Andras made a good point. The wyvern didn't have to worry about things like a fire or a bedroll.

"All right. But I'll be paying attention to how long it takes to set up camp."

His jaw tightened, and he said, "Of course, Lady Nialas."

He didn't speak again as he pulled things from the pack. It was a brownie-made pack and carried a lot more than should have fit inside it, including a bedroll and our tent. My pack included my bedroll and enough food for a week's journey.

By the time we had everything set up and a small fire started, night had truly fallen and I was grateful Andras had stopped us. I tripped over a root, landing on my face next to the fire. Andras just watched me, not getting up to offer assistance.

"Have you ever been on a journey like this before?"

"Of course not," I said, sitting up. "When Mother and Father would travel, we always had carriages. We would never go traipsing through the forest."

"Naturally not."

"Are you being snippy?"

"Of course not, my lady. I'm being sarcastic."

I blinked, unaccustomed to someone being so rude to me. Most people would pretend to be nice to me, sickly sweet in order to appear as though they liked me. I'd always been able to tell when they didn't. Andras didn't hide his annoyance.

"Why are you here if you don't want to help me?"

"Because Princess Calynn ordered me to."

"Oh." Princess Calynn. Always her. Everyone loved Calynn.

I was so lost in my own thoughts, I didn't notice Andras had removed something from his pack, a small parcel wrapped in another handkerchief. This one had a different embroidery around the edge: little snowflakes.

He removed the handkerchief to reveal a small piece of wood.

"What is that?" I asked.

"A willow branch," he replied, turning it this way and that in his hands. He paid closer attention to the wood than to me as he examined it from every angle.

"What is it for?"

He cast me an irritated glance before returning his attention to the willow. "Carving. You should eat and then rest. We'll try to get a lot of distance behind us tomorrow. Though it would be more helpful if we knew where we were going." He sent this irritated glance to Derecho, who was already dozing on his perch in the tree.

"He can't help it," I said. "He doesn't see terrain the way we do."

Andras just returned his gaze to the wood and then pulled a small knife from his pocket and began carving.

He didn't speak to me or even look at me for a long time, focused instead on carving the wood. I ate some food and left some out for him to eat as well, though he didn't touch it right away. Eventually, I crawled into the tent and lay on my bedroll, hoping sleep would allow me a bit of peace, even for just a little while.

Chapter 7

When I woke in the morning, I found myself snuggled against Andras' side. I gasped and rolled back to my side of the small tent. Had he noticed? Was he awake?

I glanced over. His breathing was even and his eyes were closed. If he was awake, he was feigning sleep well.

I shivered, suddenly cold in the winter morning. I drew my blanket around my shoulders and climbed out of the tent, stretching muscles sore from sleeping on the ground. Derecho looked up at me from his place near the final embers of the fire. He chittered a good morning, and I smiled at him before moving away to relieve myself. By the time I returned, Andras had also come out of the tent and was crouched by the fire he had built up again. He had a pan over it, cooking something while he talked to Derecho.

"Do you eat cooked meat?" he asked.

Derecho chirped at him and I knew the answer was no. I was about to tell Andras that when he responded to Derecho.

"Would you like some raw, then?"

"You understand him?" I asked, moving closer.

Andras glanced at me over his shoulder. "Some." He turned back to the fire. "We talked last night. I understand his tones. And he was kind enough to teach me yes and no."

I sat on the ground next to Andras, the smell of bacon luring me in.

"Derecho lived with me for fifteen years and no one else in Glacia bothered to learn anything about him."

He looked at me askance. "Are you comparing me to the noble daoine sidhe?"

"I'm comparing you to all the other fae I know."

"How many of them are mongrels?"

I was about to tell him a lot of mongrels lived at my father's estate and none had attempted to understand Derecho. Then I considered it and realized I hadn't introduced Derecho to any of them.

"And how many of them are lesser fae?" he continued.

I remained silent. It was the same answer, and we both knew it. I didn't need to say it out loud. He handed me a plate filled with bacon and bread. He passed a few slices of raw bacon to Derecho, who ate them greedily.

We ate, packed, and began walking. We didn't talk. Instead, I considered what he'd said. I'd spent my whole life believing I needed to fit in among the noble daoine sidhe and not quite making it work. What would have happened if I'd tried to befriend the lesser fae? Not that I ever would have. My parents raised me to believe I should be one of them, one of the noble class, even while simultaneously keeping me at arm's length.

"Calynn has a friend in the human world," I said out loud without meaning to. It had been at least an hour since Andras had asked me those questions. It was far too late to continue the conversation. He turned to me, waiting for me to continue. Though I didn't have much more to say. "Her friend is a mongrel."

He didn't say anything in response. But then, I hadn't really asked a question. What I wanted to ask was too vulnerable, too deep. I couldn't ask him if he thought I would have had friends if I'd tried to befriend a mongrel. So, we continued on in silence, only the sound of snow crunching beneath our feet and the occasional swoop from Derecho to distract me from my thoughts.

After another hour of silence, I was trying to come up with something, anything to say, when I tripped over a root poking up through the snow, falling on my face. Just like I had last night.

"Merciful Mother," I said, scrambling up and dusting myself off.

"Are you all right?" Andras asked.

"I'm fine," I said, lifting my chin, waiting for the insult to come, something that would show me exactly what he thought of my clumsiness.

"You don't have to pretend with me," he said instead. "You're not hurt?"

Warmth flooded through me at his concern. I swallowed hard and shook my head. Who was this man? Sarcastic and annoyed, but at the same time kind and concerned.

As we walked, I considered my recent behavior. I'd treated him poorly from the moment I met him because of some notion that mongrels were worth less. But hadn't the nobles treated me the same as how they treated the mongrels? Sure, they had tolerated me for my parents' sakes. None had been kind. None had done more than merely endure my presence. In fact, if I was being honest, I had been treated far better than any mongrel.

"I'm sorry," I blurted. It wasn't something said often in the Sidhe, given the implied debt that came with it. "I was terrible to you when we first met. And you have been kind to me." I found the handkerchief he'd given me in my pocket, rubbing it between my fingers.

"You should be careful with those words, Lady Nialas," he said, casting me a concerned look.

I clutched the handkerchief without drawing it out of my pocket. "I know. But I felt like I should say it. I know there's an implied debt. I will concede to anything you believe is necessary as recompense for my rudeness."

He watched me carefully, but before he could say anything, Derecho screeched and landed in front of us. He chittered and chirped. Then he took off into the sky again without looking back, as though his instructions hadn't caused the breath to catch in my throat and my heartbeat to speed.

"What did he say?" Andras asked.

"He said it's just a little further before we have to cross the water."

Andras and I stared at each other, and I could tell he was having the same reaction as I was. His eyes widened and his face drained of color.

"We have to cross the river?" he asked.

"I—I think so? He didn't say anything about crossing the river before we left. I didn't know." Of course, crossing the river for Derecho would be nothing. He could simply fly over it, well away from the kelpies and nixies. And the morgens. I shuddered to think of the creatures living in the river, all of whom would eat us at the slightest opportunity. Tears filled my eyes, and I looked around, as though trying to find another way, but if Derecho's aerie was on the other side of the river, there was no other way. "How are we going to continue? I need to be able to help Derecho's family, but I can't cross the river. I don't want to be eaten."

"Nialas," Andras said, gripping my shoulders. I turned my gaze back to him and our eyes caught. His warm brown eyes held mine, and I felt my panic dissolve. "The safest times to cross are dawn and dusk. We'll walk a little further and camp closer to the river. Can you call Derecho back?"

I did, and Andras let go of my shoulders. I wished he hadn't. The warmth of his hands had steadied me. I shoved my hand into my pocket and twisted the handkerchief around my fingers.

When Derecho landed in front of us, he tilted his head to the side questioningly.

"It's dangerous for us to cross the river," Andras explained. "Do you know a crossing point where the river is narrowest?"

Derecho chirped in the affirmative.

"Is it close? Can you take us there so we can set up camp for the night?"

Derecho chirped another yes and took off.

"You have a plan?" I asked.

"I hope so. I can probably build us a raft this evening. We'll have to work quickly if we want to have it ready for dawn."

"Do you truly think we can cross on a raft and be safe from the creatures?"

"Unless you can think of another way to cross, I think it's our only choice. My magic is flora magic, specifically trees. Though I have a bit of earth magic as well."

"Mon-" I stopped myself from saying the word and tried again. "Half human daoine sidhe have two magics?"

"Yes." He said it as though it was common knowledge. As though everyone knew this.

"So why do they treat you so poorly?" I asked, agitated. "You have the same magical strength as the rest of them."

He turned toward me, confusion marring his features. "Are you angry on my behalf?"

"I suppose I am. What's the difference between you and a full daoine sidhe?"

"Well, our life spans, for one. The full daoine sidhe live to roughly 3000 years old. I'll only live about half that time."

I snorted. "Fifteen hundred years is still a long time to me."

"As a changeling, you could live to be at least 300. Possibly longer. My father is 120 now, I believe."

"Your father is a changeling?" I asked, suddenly curious about this man, wanting to know more about him. Wanting to know everything about him.

Andras nodded, tracking Derecho as the wyvern swooped through the air before landing.

"I think our friend has found us a spot to camp," he said. "You said before you would concede to anything I believed necessary as recompense for your rudeness."

"I will," I replied cautiously.

"I would like to learn more of Derecho's language. Would you teach me?"

It hadn't been what I expected. Instead of asking for some favor that would help him rise in status, he simply asked for knowledge. What more did I need to know about him?

"Of course."

CHAPTER 8

We set up camp and Andras began pulling down large saplings, using them to create a raft to cross the river. While he worked, I had Derecho make some screeches and squawks and explained what each one meant. Even occupied as he was, Andras picked up the sounds quickly.

Night descended, and I sat near the fire as Andras put the raft together. I cooked some food, something I'd never done for another person, and brought it to him. He looked up at me, startled, and then smiled and took it. I watched him work, using his magic to bend and stretch the wood he'd harvested. We practiced a bit more of the wyvern speech and as the moon rose and cast eerie shadows, my jaw cracked in a yawn.

"Why don't you get some rest," Andras said. "I'll finish this."

"I've been little help," I said. The truth was, I might have been able to help him. I could use flora magic as well as every other element, though I'd never attempted to use it the way he was now. However, it was forbidden for humans to use magic in the Sidhe, and I couldn't expose myself, even if I was beginning to trust Andras. It also wouldn't be fair to ask him to keep my secret.

I still felt as though I wasn't helping Derecho. I would have walked blindly into darkness the first night. Now, we had to cross the river and I couldn't even help build the raft.

"Without you, we wouldn't even know there was a problem," Andras said. "You're the one Derecho trusts."

While that was true, I also knew I'd been supremely unprepared for this trip. I could do nothing about it now, so I crawled into the tent and onto my bedroll.

The ground was hard and cold. It took a long time to get comfortable, but eventually, I drifted off before Andras sought his own sleep.

When I woke in the morning, I was pressed against his side, his arm holding me there. I was so warm and content that I wanted to stay there forever.

I sat up quickly, shaken by the thought. The movement woke Andras. He rubbed his eyes.

"We should get moving. It will be dawn soon," he said, as though nothing was wrong. As though I hadn't just wanted to shimmy out of my bedroll and into his.

We got up and broke camp. Then we dragged the raft to the riverbank.

"Are you sure about this?" I asked.

"Not at all. But I can't think of another way. It would be better if Derecho could fly us over, but he's too small to carry our weight. Perhaps on the way back, his sister or her mate could, but for now, we're on our own."

He watched the eastern horizon. I watched as well as we waited for the right moment. The sky grew steadily lighter until the first rays of the sun began to peek out.

"Now," he said.

I climbed onto the raft and he maneuvered it onto the water, stepping into the river and pushing until he was up to his knees. Then he jumped on as well with a splash, a nixie already clinging to his pant leg. Derecho swooped out of the sky and plucked it off him with his clawed foot and stung it with the barb on his tail before swallowing it in one gulp.

Andras grinned at the wyvern and then took up one of the branches he had fashioned into an oar, rowing us across the river.

We'd barely gotten a quarter of the way across when Andras tugged on the oar, but it refused to come out of the water.

"What's wrong?" I asked.

"Something is holding it."

My heart raced as he struggled to continue moving us forward. Then, whatever was holding the oar yanked it from his grasp and we were suddenly adrift in the river with no way to get across. We began to float with the current.

"If we can't get across, we'll be sent out to sea," I said.

Andras laughed, a sound bordering on hysteria. "We'll never make it to the sea," he said.

He was right. A huge, black kelpie emerged from the water. The horse's head had serpents for a mane and bared teeth that could easily cut into flesh. It brayed at us and I knew it was going to eat us. I didn't think. I just lifted the river water with my magic and sent the kelpie back under the surface. It wouldn't hold for long, so I called air to push our raft and called the river to redirect the current, sailing us toward the opposite shore. The kelpie returned, behind us this time, and Andras drew his sword. The creature was impossibly fast in the water, its hooves moving through the river as though it were solid ground. Magic swept over me as the kelpie sent a flood toward us, attempting to capsize us. I held the water off with a groan and continued pushing us across the river.

We were three-quarters of the way when the kelpie reached us, the raft dipping under its weight as it climbed aboard. Andras attacked it with his sword. I was conscious of the battle behind me, but kept my focus on the magic moving us through the water. Derecho screeched as he joined the fight, using his back legs to claw at the kelpie's eyes before stinging it with his barbed tail. While his poison wouldn't act quickly on a creature of the kelpie's size, the stings made an excellent distraction. Then we were on the far bank, and I sprinted to dry land. When I was near the tree line, I turned back. Kelpies weren't as strong on land as they were in the river, so Andras and Derecho were holding their ground, slowly backing toward me. They worked well together, an intricate dance of sword and claw.

Finally, after what seemed like an eternity, the kelpie withdrew, deciding perhaps we weren't worth the fight.

Derecho chittered a victory speech and Andras laughed even though he couldn't have fully understood the wyvern. They came toward me, both breathing heavily. My gaze roved over them, checking for injuries and finding none. Then I met Andras' eyes.

I'd used magic. Which wasn't allowed. I licked my lips and swallowed, waiting for him to remark on it.

He stared at me for a moment, the exuberance of the successful fight draining from him. I wanted to scream as I waited for him to condemn me. His face gave away none of his thoughts until he said, "We should get moving. We have a long way to go."

He started walking, and I scurried after him.

"You're not..." I trailed off, not sure if I should say the words out loud.

He turned to me, waiting.

"You won't say anything?"

"Say anything about what? How you saved our lives?"

I blinked back the tears of relief. "Right. That."

"I won't say anything, Lady Nialas."

We walked in silence for a little while. Then I said, "You can just call me Nialas. If you want."

He gave me a smile and butterflies swarmed my belly. I smiled back.

CHAPTER 9

We walked and walked and by the time Andras said it was time to set up camp, my feet were killing me. I took off my shoes and rubbed them by the fire before I crawled into my bedroll and fell asleep faster than ever before.

For the third day, I woke up in Andras' arms, snuggled against his warmth. I was too tired to move quickly away from him. If I was being honest with myself, I also didn't want to. He was warm and strong and smart. He was sexy and kind.

My breath caught in my throat and my heart beat heavy in my chest. I liked him. And that was the scariest thing I had ever thought. Because, while I had liked people before, no one had ever liked me back. What if Andras didn't either?

"What's wrong?" Andras asked.

I gasped and sat up. "You're awake?"

He nodded and reached out to wipe away a tear that had escaped. "What's wrong?"

"Nothing," I lied. "I'm just tired. We should get started."

I climbed out of the tent and he let me go. After a moment spent composing myself, I found some food for us to eat while Andras rolled up our bedrolls and put away the tent. When he finished, I handed him the food, and he took it with a smile. I loved that smile. The way he looked at me like I was useful. Like he wanted me around.

I hesitated, thinking of the question swarming my mind since he'd reacted so calmly to me being pressed against him this morning. I swallowed, working up the courage to ask if he'd known we snuggled together each morning.

"It looks like we're going to be hiking up the mountain today," he said before I could ask anything. "Are you ready for this?"

I blinked up at the mountain in front of us, my question receding to the back of my mind. The peak reached up into the sky, surrounded by clouds.

"We have to climb that?" I glanced between Andras and Derecho. The wyvern squawked the affirmative. My feet ached just thinking about it.

We finished packing up and started.

"We probably won't make it as far today as yesterday or the day before," Andras said. "We'll have to go slower. But I spoke with Derecho last night and he said it's not too far up the mountain."

"You spoke with Derecho last night?"

"Yes. Before we switched watch."

"Switched watch?"

He gave me a bemused smile. "You think all three of us are sleeping at once? I stay awake for the first few hours and then Derecho takes the second shift so I can sleep."

"Why don't you ask me to keep watch?"

"You need more sleep. You're not used to such long, arduous treks. I'd rather you rested so we can keep making good time. I'm used to not getting much sleep."

While it galled that he accurately noted I wasn't used to such rough conditions, I had to admit it was true. Self-doubt still flared within me, forcing me to ask the question despite fearing the answer.

"So it's not because you don't think I could handle keeping watch?"

"No, Nialas. You've proven yourself capable."

Derecho screeched, interrupting our conversation. We started up the mountain path he pointed out and I stopped talking, struggling to breathe after just a short time. My legs burned, and we stopped frequently to drink water. It made me angry every time we stopped. I wanted to get to the aerie today. Who knew how many eggs had been stolen in the days we had been walking? But Andras insisted.

"If we push too hard," he said, "you could hurt yourself. Then it will take twice as long to get back. We're making good time."

"You're not even breathing hard. How is it so easy for you?"

"It's not that easy. I recover faster because I've been training every day for a long time. You haven't."

"I wasn't really prepared for this, was I?"

He gave me a lopsided smile. "Not exactly. But you're doing really well. And knowing what Derecho is saying has been vital. I couldn't have done this without you."

We kept going until Andras said it was time to set up camp. I sat down on the ground immediately.

"Get up," he said.

"I just need to rest for a minute. Then I'll help with camp."

"Don't worry about camp. You need to stretch or else you'll be too stiff to move tomorrow."

He led me through a few stretches, helping me with my balance, even though a tree stood right next to us. Did he want to touch me as much as I wanted to touch him? He sat me down and showed me a few more stretches that included twisting, showing me how I should move, his fingers lingering on my shoulder or my knee as I twisted and stretched. He skimmed his fingers along the muscles I was supposed to be stretching, and every time he did, my skin tingled. By the time we were done, I was out of breath. He was sitting close to me, his brown eyes peering into mine. His gaze dropped to my lips, and I felt myself drifting closer to him.

He cleared his throat. "Camp and then food," he declared, standing up. He set up the tent quickly and placed our bedrolls inside.

Derecho chirped and chittered, and I turned my attention to him.

"Did he say we should be there tomorrow?" Andras asked.

"Yes. He said we're close now. About three quarters of the way."

Derecho chirped again, and I shot him a look.

"He said he wants to go to the aerie and check on his sister. He'll be back in the morning."

Andras nodded and Derecho flew off.

"You can't stay awake all night," I said.

He shrugged as he poked the fire, then began cooking some meat over it. "Won't be the first time. Derecho needs to know his sister is still doing well. It'll be good for him to tell her we're almost there so she and her mate can get ready for the journey. We discussed it last night."

"You knew he was going?"

"I knew it was possible. If we didn't make it to the aerie today, he was going to go."

"Why didn't you say so?"

"It's fine, Nialas," he said, his tone reassuring. "It's only one night. I'll be all right."

I drew my knees up as I waited for him to finish cooking and then took the plate gratefully. Andras sat next to me, his side pressed into mine. I realized, in addition to being concerned for him, I was sad I wouldn't get to wake up in his arms again.

"Maybe I should stay awake tonight as well?"

"You need rest. Derecho said tomorrow night he and his sister's mate would stay awake so I could sleep the whole night."

"You've picked up his language really quickly."

"I pay attention."

"So I've noticed."

We fell into a comfortable silence for a while until Andras said, "You should get to sleep."

I nodded, but didn't move. "Perhaps I could stay awake with you for a little while. To keep you company?"

He turned toward me with another beautiful smile. "I'd like that."

He rummaged in his bag and pulled out the willow branch and a knife. Whatever he was making had started to take shape.

"You've done all that in just a few nights?" I asked.

"I like to carve," he said simply.

I reached over to trace the line along the top. "Is it a bird?"

"I think Derecho would take offense at that," he said.

"It's Derecho?"

"It was supposed to be a wyvern, not him specifically. But the more I do, the more I see it's him. He's got a bit of an arrogant personality, but with a vulnerability when he thinks no one is looking."

"It's beautiful." My fingers traced over the line of the wing again and then drifted over his fingers. I wished I could take his hand in mine, lean in and kiss him. But the idea he might not want me as much as I wanted him terrified me. I let my hand drop.

"Nialas," he said, his voice husky.

I lifted my eyes back to his, searching, hoping. Hyper-aware of his arm and leg pressed against mine. My heartbeat thundered in my chest.

"Andras," I whispered, afraid to say anything too loud and break the spell.

One of his hands lifted to touch my face, his thumb sweeping across my cheekbone. My eyes drifted closed. "You've never said my name before," he said.

"I haven't?"

"No." His fingers trailed along my jaw and curled around the back of my neck. He didn't pull me closer, just held me in place. "Did you know when I come into the tent each night, I'm barely settled before you roll toward me?"

I shook my head.

"I thought you perhaps just wanted the warmth, but now I wonder if it's more than that."

"Andras, I—" But I didn't know what to say. Pretending to come on to Ronan had been easy. There were no emotions involved. Here, with Andras, I couldn't help but wonder if he wanted me or if he looked at me and saw Calynn. Just like my parents had always done. Just like everyone had always done.

"Whatever you're thinking now, stop," he said.

"What do you mean?"

"You're hurting yourself. Stop it. I can see the pain in your eyes. I don't want it there when I kiss you."

"You're going to kiss me?" I asked, breathless.

"Do you want me to?"

I couldn't say any words, so I simply nodded.

He lowered his head and my eyes drifted closed. His lips touched mine softly, and I melted into him. His arms folded around me and he deepened the kiss, his tongue sweeping into my mouth and sending desire flooding through me. I wanted this man more than I had ever wanted anything. It was terrifying, but I pushed the terror away. I would take everything he was willing to give me and deal with the fallout later.

I turned my body toward him, and he lifted me onto his lap so I straddled him. My arms twined around his neck and my fingers buried into his hair. He held me close, in a way no one had held me before, as though I was precious.

My hands drifted across his broad shoulders, down his sides to where his shirt tucked into his pants. I started to tug, but he stopped me.

I lifted my head to look at him, my terror returning.

"I'm not going to take you to bed on the ground, Nialas," he said, pulling me closer so he could kiss me again. "And you need to rest. We still have a long way to go." But he didn't let me go to find my sleep. He just kept kissing me, and I didn't want him to ever stop.

CHAPTER 10

When I woke the next morning, I was snuggled against Andras once again, one of his strong arms holding me to him. I stretched and looked up at him. He was awake, his other arm folded under his head. When he felt me move, he turned his attention from the roof of the tent to me.

"I thought you weren't going to sleep," I said.

"I didn't. But after you'd been in here for a few hours, I figured I could stay awake in here just as easily as out there."

He captured my lips with his and I rolled so I was lying half on him and half off. I wanted to keep going, see where this would lead, but I heard a familiar chittering outside the tent and reluctantly pulled away.

"Derecho is back," I said.

He pulled my lips back to his for a swift, hard kiss and then let me go. I packed up the tent and bedrolls as Andras cooked us some food. Then it was time for us to go. We started walking, and Andras linked his fingers through mine. I glanced down at our hands but didn't remark on it, trying to contain my stupid smile.

The path quickly became steep, and we had to let go out of practicality. It didn't take long to reach the aerie, but the last stretch required a scramble up a steep embankment. Then we stared into the glittering black eyes of a huge golden wyvern.

"Hello," I said. "We're Derecho's friends. We've come to help move your eggs."

Another huge head lifted, this one scarlet, half hidden behind the golden one.

Her beak parted and she let out a loud screech.

"I'm the one who found Derecho's egg," I explained. "Did he not tell you about me?"

She chirped and the golden wyvern stood from the nest. He was bigger than a buggane. His barbed tail whipped around and pointed at me.

Andras pushed me aside and held out his hands.

"You asked for help."

Derecho's sister chirped again.

"We were sent by the White Hart," I shouted.

Everyone stilled. Derecho screeched and launched himself at his sister, beating her face with his wings. She shook her head and the tension of the moment faded. I considered what I needed to be in this moment. A confident woman who knew what she was talking about and what we needed to do. I also needed, as much as it pained me, to be an advocate for Calynn's abilities.

"I understand you're frightened," I said. "Derecho mentioned you didn't want your mate hunting, so you probably haven't eaten in the days since Derecho has been gone. But we're going to help you move your nest and everything will be all right. My sister owns a property not far from here. She has the Stag's blessing. She said you can create a new nest on her property and she will help keep you safe."

The golden wyvern spoke for the first time, chittering derisively.

"The Stag doesn't give his blessing to just anyone," I shot back. "She's a daoine sidhe who recently competed in the Winter Solstice challenges and passed each one to the third task. She's strong enough to protect what's hers. And if you have your nest on her land, she would consider you hers."

He chirped again.

"Yes, it was recent. She's young. But if she says she can keep you safe, she will."

I waited as the wyverns considered.

"You asked Derecho to find you help. He did. Now it's up to you to accept it."

Derecho's sister chirped in assent, and Andras relaxed. We gathered the remaining eggs, wrapping three in my bedroll and three in Andras' bedroll, then tucking them into our packs. Finally, we began making our way down the mountain. The trek down was more difficult than the climb had been, and I found myself holding on to Andras for balance more often than not.

Every few hours, Derecho's sister screeched at us to stop and take the eggs out, creating a nest for her on the ground to brood them. During these times, Andras insisted I stretch before I sat down, gently helping me into the right positions to avoid injury, his touch lingering as he did, causing heat to bloom within me and desire to pool in my core. He stayed close, whether we were walking or resting. I knew he must be exhausted after the long night, but he didn't show it. When we made it back to the base of the mountain where we'd camped two nights before, he called us all to stop.

The golden wyvern screeched in protest, but Andras held up his hands without me having to translate.

"Lady Nialas and I can't walk through the dark. We all need to rest. And it's colder at night so we'd have to stop more frequently to warm up the eggs. Best to set up camp and let your mate brood through the night."

Derecho chirped his agreement, and they discussed who would keep watch. Derecho explained how he had promised to let Andras sleep this night and then, moving forward, they would split the watch between the three of them. When it was all sorted, we set up camp, and I made food. Derecho hunted for his sister and her mate. Then Andras and I went into the tent together.

"You understood what he said?" I asked as we lay down. It felt so right to lie beside him, his arms holding me close, my head resting on his chest with his heart beating beneath my ear. A ridiculous amount of happiness filled me with the knowledge that he would get to stay with me all night. I tried to ignore the swooping in my belly at the thought of what might happen between us.

"I didn't have to," Andras said. "I understood the tone just fine." He paused as his hand started drifting along my spine, drifting up and down. "You spoke kindly of the princess today. I admit, I was surprised."

"It could be I was wrong about her." I thought back to what Ronan had told me about his role in my being changed. "I blamed her for everything wrong in my life. But she didn't have any more choice in the matter than I did." I paused. "Do you remember when I mentioned her friend in the human world?"

"You did, and you never explained why."

"I've never made any friends, save Derecho. My parents insisted I spend my time with the other noble daoine sidhe and none of them ever cared about me. Do you think, if I had tried to be kinder to those who are half human, could I have made friends with them?"

I looked up and found his warm brown eyes.

"I think changelings and mongrels are more alike than not. The fae sense the human in us and don't want us. We tend to live in a world between. Not exactly fae, but not exactly human, either."

His fingers trailing over my back sent tingles through my whole body. I wiggled a little closer to him and he chuckled before kissing me. I slid my hand along his chest and down, but he caught it before I could touch the area of his body I wanted. He nipped my lip lightly.

"I'm still not taking you to bed on the ground. Not for the first time. You deserve more than that, Nialas. We have time."

I'd never understood what it meant to have someone's heart skip a beat before. In that moment, I did. It felt like the whole world stopped and restarted and a single thought became crystal clear in my mind. I didn't just like this man.

I loved him.

My heart restarted at an accelerated pace, and I pulled his lips to mine. His hands tightened around me as his tongue dipped into my mouth and danced with mine.

"I want you," I whispered, unable to make the declaration any louder.

"I can tell." He shifted, pressing his erection against my thigh. "I want you, too."

"Why should we wait?"

"It'll be better this way. I promise."

I felt the magic of the words close around us, binding him to his word. Binding me. Something in me eased. I kissed him again, softer this time, and then relaxed against him. His fingers continued the soft drag along my spine, up and down, in a soothing rhythm, until I fell asleep.

Chapter 11

The next day passed much the same. We stopped every few hours to allow Derecho's sister to brood the clutch of eggs. Andras and I walked together companionably. We talked and shared little touches, a hand on the shoulder here, a nudge with an elbow there. When we stopped, we sat close together. He brought out his carving each time and whittled a little more. I watched in awe as the tiny statue came to life.

We camped on the shore of the river and the golden wyvern said he could fly us over in the morning. I slept easily, knowing we wouldn't have a repeat of the initial crossing. Derecho carried the bags over while the golden wyvern lifted me easily. It was uncomfortable, but he held me high above the water. He set me down gently on the other side and then returned for Andras.

Derecho's sister flew behind them, spotting. Andras was larger than I was and heavier. The wyverns were large and certainly able to carry him, but I still watched with my heart in my throat, the handkerchief he had given me twisted in my hands. They didn't fly quite as high as they did with me, and a tentacle reached out of the water toward Andras' dangling feet. I gasped, but the wyvern beat his huge wings, lifting them both out of reach, and the tentacle disappeared beneath the waves again.

Then they were on the bank and I couldn't stop myself from rushing to Andras, wrapping my arms around him, letting his solidity ease the fear that had eaten me. He chuckled as his arms came around me, stroking my back again, the slow rhythm soothing me.

"Everything is fine," he said.

"When that tentacle came up, I thought it was going to pull you down."

"It didn't even touch me."

The golden wyvern screeched, and I stepped back long before I was ready to. We retrieved our packs from Derecho, shrugging them on and continuing. Andras took my hand, squeezing my fingers. He didn't let go and my anxiety finally eased.

We talked more. Andras told me about how his mother cast him out when he was only fifteen years old, against his father's wishes. Since his father was a changeling and human, he had no say in the matter. I told him about my parents and how they only seemed to care about me when I could be a symbol for something.

When we stopped for the night, Andras took the first watch. I tossed and turned, trying to sleep, but finding it elusive. It took until he climbed into the space next to me to realize I had been waiting for him. The thought was unsettling. How would I fall asleep when we returned to our regular lives? How would I ever go back to my life when he left me?

With the soft rhythm of his fingers stroking along my spine easing me to sleep, I couldn't bring myself to worry.

By the end of the next day, we were back at the spot where we had camped the first night, and I was exhausted. The almost constant walking and carrying the eggs had been a lot in the last few days. I hadn't expected the wyvern eggs to be so heavy, but they weighed almost ten pounds each. Given how big Derecho had been when he hatched, I shouldn't have been surprised, but that had been twenty years ago.

"We'll be back at Calynn's property tomorrow," I said as Andras and I sat by the fire in the evening. We'd already cooked and eaten dinner.

He nodded, watching as the mother wyvern nestled herself over her clutch and closed her eyes. I'd started calling her Cirrus and him Cyclone during the last day—him after the low-pressure system that brings unsettled weather including hurricanes, and her after the soft clouds usually associated with fair weather, but which could also herald a storm. Since their true wyvern names were unpronounceable with our tongues, they agreed to these names.

It hadn't been a difficult journey for neither Cirrus nor Cyclone, but I knew it had to be stressful, leaving your home to start new in a place you simply had to trust would be safe. We were all feeling tired.

I rubbed my aching legs, but it did nothing to dispel the ache lingering in them. The movement caught Andras' attention, and he gestured toward our small tent. "Let's go to bed."

"You're not taking first watch tonight?"

"I'm taking last."

"So you won't be there when I wake up?"

He smiled. "Will you miss me?"

Yes. "Of course not. I'll be asleep."

The truth was, I had quickly become accustomed to waking in his arms, starting the day with a long, slow kiss. I wanted every day to start that way.

"Of course," he said, grinning now. "How silly of me."

After we slid into the tent, Andras had me lay on my stomach. He settled over me and began rubbing my back in a gentle massage.

"If it wasn't so cold, I'd tell you to take off your clothes. It would be better if I could touch your skin."

My stomach flipped at the combination of his words and hands. I wanted so badly to turn over and take both of our clothes off. Take this intense desire to where we wanted it to go. Instead, I stayed, remembering his promise a few nights before. How it would be better if we waited for a bed than if we slept together on the ground. Now that it was just one more night, I was eager to get there. But which bed would we find? He lived in the barracks with the other guards. There wouldn't be much, if any, privacy there. So we'd have to go to mine. Which meant he would have to come up to the second floor of Calynn's house, where very few people went. She hadn't forbidden people from going up, but most guards didn't venture where they weren't posted. And Ronan hadn't posted any guards on the second floor.

"What's going to happen when we return to Calynn's home?" I asked.

His hands had drifted down my back to begin massaging my thighs. "We'll have to get the wyverns settled. I may need to debrief the marshal on what happened."

"Then what? Will you come to my room?"

"Do you want me to?"

I turned under him before he could reach my calves and gripped his shirt in both of my hands, pulling him down toward me. He came without resistance, following my movement. I kissed him hard, and he responded in kind, sweeping his tongue into my mouth. I arched against him, holding him close to me. In only a few seconds, I felt like I was on fire. I wanted him between my thighs, but his legs still straddled mine. And we were both far more dressed than we should have been.

I pressed kisses along his jaw until my lips reached his ear. Then, I whispered, "I want you now."

"We've waited this long. We can wait one more night." He lifted his head so he could look into my eyes. "I want to do this right, Nialas. I want to take my time and spend all night focused on nothing but you. I don't want to be distracted by what could be outside this tent." He grinned wickedly and kissed my neck. My eyes closed as the feeling sent shivers through my body. "And I don't want a bunch of wyverns outside listening to what I'm doing to you."

The heat in my core exploded, and I writhed under him. He kept me trapped between his legs, his chest pinning me down. I could feel the evidence of his desire pressing into me and I wanted to open to him, invite him in, but he kept me still, kissing me until my lips were swollen. Then he slid off me and pulled the blanket around us, holding me close. His hand swept up and down my spine in a familiar gesture.

My heart still pounded with unsatisfied desire. This time, he let my hand drift down his chest to rest on the hardness I craved. I stroked him through his pants and his regular, smooth sweeps along my spine became jerky. His other hand tilted my chin up so he could look into my eyes.

"You are testing my resolve."

A smile spread across my lips before he captured them with his own. I continued stroking him, at turns rubbing gently and then firmer, until he groaned and pulled my hand away, breaking the kiss.

"Enough."

He placed my hand on his chest, with his hand over top. I could feel his heart thundering as he tried to control his breathing. I watched as he fought for control and the idea that he wanted me as much as I wanted him stoked my desire even further. After a while, he let out a sigh and placed a kiss on my hair.

"Sleep. We'll revisit this tomorrow night."

I settled my head on his shoulder, drifting in contentment as the now familiar beating of his heart lulled me into my dreams.

CHAPTER 12

We pushed through the next day, stopping less frequently as the end of our journey came closer. I could admit I wanted to get there partly so I could find time to be with Andras. But I also wanted to see the wyverns settled.

Calynn met us at the edge of her property, Ronan standing close, his massive sword resting on his shoulder, ready to defend her if necessary.

"Welcome," she said, speaking to the wyverns. "We've been preparing for your arrival. If you'll follow me, I'll show you to the spot."

I fell into step beside her as we walked.

"How was the trip?" she asked with what seemed to be genuine interest.

I glanced at Andras without consciously deciding to do so. "It was good. I'm tired. Not used to so much walking. There was some trouble crossing the river, but we managed all right. The wyverns flew us across on the way back."

"Good." We walked in silence for a few minutes. "Your debt is repaid, Nialas. You need to decide what you want to do next."

My step hesitated for a moment. "I just thought you would want to keep me here."

"I have no claim on you anymore. If you want to stay, it's your choice. You're welcome here. But you're a free woman."

My heart raced at the thought that I could do anything. There were too many possibilities. Which option would I choose? Did I want to stay here? Did I want to return to Glacia? If I returned to the city, what would I do?

And if I returned to Glacia, who would I be leaving behind?

We arrived at the spot where Calynn had set up a space for the wyverns—a large cliff face with a ledge about fifty feet up. I didn't remember the cliff from my walks around the property before.

"Has this always been here?" I asked.

Calynn shook her head. "I did some research on wyvern aeries. I didn't have any terrain like that here, so I made this."

"You created a mountain with a cliff in the last week?" I asked, incredulous.

"Well, I had some help. Ronan's latent magic is bedrock, so he helped me find it. I just did the heavy lifting. Literally."

She said it like it was no big deal, like anyone could do it. I looked between her and the new mountain, my jaw dropped open. She wasn't paying attention to me. While we talked, Cyclone had flown up to the ledge and then back down, chittering to his mate and then to us.

"Whatever materials you need to make it comfortable, let me know and I'll help you," Calynn said. "There should be space for your hoard up there as well. If you need more, let me know."

"We didn't bring their hoard," I said. "Between the three of them, they have quite a collection of precious gems and we couldn't carry it. So we just brought the eggs."

She nodded. "The eggs are the most important. But I'm sure they'll want to go back for the hoard, eventually."

Cirrus chirped, and I pulled the first two eggs from my pack. She took them carefully, one in each clawed foot, and carried them up to the ledge.

Then she flew down for the next ones. One more trip had all six eggs where they belonged and she settled in to brood them. I could see her nudging them with her beak until they were sitting just right.

We left the wyverns to their tasks and began the walk back to Calynn's house.

"I can have Ethna bring you water for a bath," Calynn said. "I remember how dirty I felt after weeks traipsing through the forest."

I hadn't noticed the grime of travel until she brought up the idea of a bath. Now that she had, I wanted nothing more than to scrub the dirt and sweat from my body.

"That would be amazing."

"You seem different," she said, eyeing me carefully. "More... relaxed?"

I couldn't stop myself from looking at Andras again. He was walking next to Ronan, deep in discussion about something. Probably telling the marshal all the details of our journey. It made me think about the details he wouldn't mention. The kisses, the touches, the promises. My heartbeat quickened.

I shrugged. "I don't feel any different," I responded.

Calynn laughed out loud, rolling her eyes and grinning at me. "Whatever you say, Nialas."

She continued walking as I stopped and stared after her, remembering belatedly that she could hear it when I lied.

***

The bath was bliss. I scrubbed my skin until it was pink and then washed my hair twice. By the time I was done, the water had cooled. I climbed out, drying off and finding a simple chemise to wear while I combed the tangles out of my hair. It was something a maid used to do, but I found delight in doing it for myself. I could do a lot of things for myself now. Calynn had said I was free to do whatever I wanted. I could go anywhere. Do anything.

Be with anyone.

Someone knocked softly on my door. I found a robe and went to answer it. When I opened the door, my stomach flipped and then filled with butterflies. Andras had also cleaned up and looked gorgeous in fresh clothes, his hair combed back, his brown eyes filled with heat as he took me in.

"The marshal gave me the evening off. I don't start my shifts again until tomorrow."

"That's good. You've had a long few days."

"So have you. You're probably tired." He shifted from one foot to the other as though he wasn't sure whether he should stay or go. He glanced around. "There aren't any guards posted on this floor. I've only been up here a couple of times."

"It's family only." I stepped out of the room and pointed to the door on the far end. "That's Calynn's room. Her maid, Quinn, sleeps there. The boy, Rhys, sleeps there." I pointed to each door in turn. "That's supposed to be Ronan's room, but I'm not sure how much he actually sleeps in there."

"He doesn't," Andras said with confidence.

I thought back to my attempt to deceive Ronan over a week ago and wondered how many people knew they were together. Was I the only one who hadn't seen what was right in front of me?

I turned back to my room. "This one is mine. Would you like to come in?"

I didn't wait for an answer and just walked back into the room. I felt a little jittery, excited and nervous about what might finally happen.

Andras followed me in, the door closing softly behind him. I took in the room, trying to see it from his eyes. It was smaller than the rooms I had at Queran's estate in Glacia. I didn't have much. The bed was large and comfortable. My stuffed bear, Baby Brother Ted, sat on the table beside the bed. The books I'd brought with me from Glacia stacked on a small desk.

"It isn't as lavish as the suite in Queran's estate," I said.

He watched me, his head tilted. "But you like it better."

I hesitated. "I think so? Everything in here is mine. Calynn said my debt is paid. I can do whatever I want now. I can go anywhere."

"Where will you go?"

"I think I'll stay here. Derecho is here now. He's my only..." I hesitated, looking at Andras, wondering if I was wrong, "He's my friend. So it would be nice to be near him again. And Calynn is maybe not as bad as I originally thought."

"Maybe," he said with a suppressed smile.

"I've been thinking about doing what you recommended and asking her to send for the rest of my books. Maybe get a bookcase in here so I don't have to barge into the library anymore."

He lost the battle against the smile. "That's very prudent of you."

We lapsed into silence, and I felt awkward, overcome with insecurities. Here we were, alone in my room, my bed right there. How did I get us there? Did he still want to be with me?

"I guess you probably want to go to bed?" I said, casting my gaze around the room, looking at everything but him.

"I do," he said.

"Oh."

I stared at the floor, uncertain, watching his boots as they came closer to me. He touched my chin, gently tilting my head so I would look at him. "Nialas. I meant I want to go to bed with you."

I couldn't breathe from the desire flooding me. My whole body ached to touch and be touched. I swayed toward him as though he was a magnet. His hand drifted along my jaw and around to cup my neck, his other arm sliding around my waist until we were pressed together. My arms settled around his shoulders, my fingers slipping into his damp hair.

"I guess you probably want to go to bed," he whispered.

A smile tugged at my lips. "I do."

Finally, finally, he leaned his head down and kissed me.

It started as a gentle press of lips, a soft promise of things to come. Then his tongue swept into my mouth and he pulled me tighter against him. His hand slid into my hair and tightened, pulling gently until my head tilted back. His lips left mine to trail kisses along the column of my throat. He took a step, not breaking contact as we made our way to my bed. My legs hit the mattress and he let me go. I made a sound of protest and reached for him, but his hands were already on me again, sliding the robe from my shoulders.

"You're going to let me take your clothes off this time?" I asked.

"I'm going to be rather upset with you if you don't."

I tugged at the hem of his shirt, pulling it out from where it tucked into his pants. Then, for the first time, I touched the skin of his stomach. I could feel the ridges of muscles as my fingers skimmed upward. It was suddenly very real. We were going to go through with it this time. My hands started to shake. His shirt was buttoned so I couldn't pull it over his head. I felt awkward for not thinking of this. I started with the bottom button, thought better of it, and moved to the top. He watched me work, but I avoided his gaze.

"Nialas, look at me," he commanded.

I raised my eyes.

"What's making you uncomfortable? You've done this before, right?"

I swallowed. "Yes."

"But?"

I looked away, trying to think of what to say. He touched my cheek, gently urging my eyes back to his.

"You don't have to hide from me," he said.

Something in me eased. The whole journey to the aerie and the whole way back, I hadn't hid or pretended to be something I wasn't. I didn't have to resume that now. Not with Andras.

"The others I've been with haven't really cared about what I want. They only took what they wanted from me. Then it was over."

"You think I'm going to be the same?" he asked. I could hear the incredulity and hurt in his voice.

"No. I think you're different from everyone I've ever met. That's what's making me nervous. If you were just like everyone else, I'd know what to do. But you're not."

He laughed. "So you're worried about how good it's going to be?"

"I'm worried I'm not going to be enough," I said as quietly as I could. I hadn't wanted to say the words out loud, but he'd said I didn't have to hide from him, and I didn't want to.

His hands framed my face, and he pressed a soft kiss against my lips. "Impossible."

Then he took my hands and guided them to his top button. I undid the first one, then the second, and the third. That was enough for him to pull the shirt over his head. I ran my hands over his abs and chest. His hands slipped down my sides, gathering my chemise, pulling it up until he had the hem bunched in his fists.

"May I?" he asked.

"Yes," I whispered.

He kissed me again before pulling my chemise over my head, leaving me naked before him. His gaze roved over me, from the top of my head to my toes. I waited for him to say something about how small I was—my size had always marked me as something less than the daoine sidhe. He just looked at me with desire and tenderness.

"You are so beautiful," he said as he gathered me against him.

My breasts crushed against his chest and I moaned at the feeling of his skin against mine. My hands found the top of his pants and I undid them, pushing them down, needing to feel more of him. He kicked off his boots as his fingers dragged up my spine in that familiar rhythm he had honed over the past few nights. The feeling settled my remaining nerves, and I kissed him hard, pressing against him.

I sat on the edge of the bed and tried to pull him down with me, but he resisted. I let him go, intending to ask what was wrong, when my gaze caught on the erection standing out toward me.

"Merciful Mother," I breathed, lifting my hands to run my fingers along his length.

His eyes drifted closed for a second and his breathing became ragged. Then he shook his head and pulled my hand away.

"Not yet," he said. "I made a promise. I intend to keep it. Now lie back."

I did as he demanded, feeling exposed with my legs hanging over the edge of the bed. He stood between them and I thought he would enter me right then. Instead, he dropped to his knees on the floor. He dragged the fingers of each hand along my legs, from the tops of my thighs, down the underside of each knee, over my calves, to cup my feet in his hands.

He lifted them onto the bed, spreading my legs wide. Then he looked up at me and stood again. He grabbed a pillow and placed it under my head.

"I want you to watch," he said, his voice making my body quiver in anticipation.

"Watch what?" I asked, surprised I had any breath at all to speak.

He smiled and dropped to his knees again.

"Perfect."

He dipped his head and kissed my core. I jerked in surprise.

"Andras, what are you—"

He pinned me in place with his brown gaze. "Do you trust me?"

My heart raced in my chest. I couldn't catch my breath. I trembled as I waited for what he was going to do next, the confidence in his eyes telling me he was going to take me somewhere I had never been. I nodded.

"Good." He bit the inside of my thigh, sending a spark of pleasure arcing to my core. "Keep your eyes on me. When I look up, I want to see you watching."

He bent his head and spread my lips with his fingers. Then he found the bundle of nerves at my center with his tongue. My eyes closed, and I lifted my hips toward his face at the first touch.

He lifted his head again and bit the inside of my other thigh.

"Eyes open, my lady."

I couldn't breathe. But I obeyed. I settled my hips again and opened my eyes as his dark head lowered once more. His hot tongue lapped and licked at my flesh and every once in a while, he glanced up to find me watching him, the erotic looks sending me higher and higher. I fought to control my breathing and my sounds, my moans coming faster and louder against my intentions. He continued his relentless ministrations and my body tightened, hovering on the brink of something I didn't understand. He lifted his head a fraction and said, "Let go, Nialas. I've got you."

He slid a finger effortlessly inside me and teased me with his tongue again until the tightness shattered in a shuddering wave of pleasure. I moaned as the shuddering ratcheted higher. His finger moved in and out of me, joined by a second and his lips closed around my nub as he sucked on it, turning my moan into a scream I smothered with my hand.

When I couldn't stand any more, I twisted my hips away and he let me go, slowly sliding his fingers out of me. He stood and sat next to me on the bed, drawing his fingers softly around one breast and then the other. I trembled under the touch as the pleasure that had swamped me evened out.

"You closed your eyes at the end," he admonished. "I'll let it slide since it was your first time."

A strangled laugh escaped me. "That's very benevolent of you."

He lay down next to me, stretching out, pulling my legs over his. "I can be."

"So that's what that feels like," I said, breathless.

He grinned. "That's what it feels like. And this is what it tastes like." He held his fingers out to me and I took them into my mouth, watching as his eyes blazed with want as my tongue licked the moisture from him. He took his hand back and replaced it with his mouth, the same sweet taste on his tongue.

I reached between us to grip his erection, sliding my hand up and down, eliciting a groan from him.

"You're trying to rush me," he said. "There's more I want to accomplish tonight."

He pulled his hips out of my reach and I tried to move toward him, but he stopped me. Instead, he helped me adjust so I was fully on the bed, stretching my legs out. Again, I waited for him to settle between my thighs and enter me, but he stayed beside me, caressing me gently. His head dipped again. This time, his lips closed over one of my nipples and I gasped. He bit gently and licked and sucked. His hand held my other breast and his fingers pinched the nipple, rolling it and sending shock waves of pleasure through my body. His other hand threaded into my hair, holding me still. I tried to reach for him again, but he wasn't close enough.

"Andras," I complained. "I need you."

"You'll have me. In time."

The hand playing with my nipple moved down, skimming through the wet cleft he had so recently ravished. I moaned again as he grazed the flesh slowly, teasing me with the lightest of touches. I was so sensitive it didn't take long for my body to begin tightening again the way it had before. My eyes drifted closed as he brought me higher with his mouth on my breast and his fingers stroking me, causing molten need to fill me. I was so close to shattering again when he lifted his head.

"Open your eyes and look at me," he commanded.

My eyes flew open and locked onto his. His pupils were dilated so only a slim ring of brown circled the black. This time, when the orgasm rocked me, I kept my eyes anchored to his. My moans gained volume, and he captured them with his mouth. He stopped stroking me, but kept his hand there as though he couldn't bring himself to let me go. I ached to have him inside me.

My body felt heavy as the pleasure pooled.

"You're amazing," I said. "This is amazing. No wonder people like to have sex so much."

He chuckled as he kissed my shoulder. "We haven't had sex yet. That was just the beginning, sweetheart."

"Well, what are we waiting for?"

"Give a woman a couple orgasms and suddenly she's ravenous for them."

I laughed as I turned, draping my body over his, setting my head on my hand so I could look at him. I would never tire of looking at him. "What *are* we waiting for, Andras? You haven't let me touch you. I want to touch you."

His hand drifted to my back to sweep along my spine. "It isn't about me," he said. "Seeing you coming apart at my hands is incredible. When we get to the sex, I'll find my pleasure then. But you said no one before had ever cared about what you want. They took from you and then were gone. You deserve to have this time be about you alone."

I refused to let the tears that pricked my eyes fall. To cover my emotional response, I reached up and kissed him, closing my eyes as I lost myself in him. He stroked his tongue over mine and tightened his hold on me. Then he moved me off him so I was lying on my back. He broke the kiss for a moment and slid a pillow beneath my hips, lifting them toward him.

"Watch," he said.

My breath caught as he kneeled between my legs, holding my hips steady as he positioned himself at my entrance.

"Ready?"

I nodded.

Slowly, he pushed inside, spreading me until I felt full. Then he pressed a little deeper. He moved in slow increments, letting me adjust to the size of him. My breathing was ragged as I watched him disappear inside me, little by little. After an eternity, he had disappeared completely.

"Eyes on me, sweetheart," he said.

He stared down at me as he began to move, his gaze heavy-lidded. The fire in his eyes stoked the fire in me and I lost every ounce of self-consciousness I had been feeling. He looked at me like I was the most beautiful creature in all the worlds.

He drew back, adjusted his hips, and thrust into me again. I gasped as he hit a spot deep within me I hadn't known was there, electric shocks sizzling across my nerves.

He gave me a sly grin. "There it is."

He moved again, setting a steady rhythm I tried to match. I had no leverage, though, so I could do little more than grip his wrists where he held my hips in place. Then he pulled one hand away, his thumb coming to rest on that little bundle of nerves once again. My eyes rolled back.

"Look at me," he demanded.

I tried to focus again, but with so much pleasure pulsing through me, I could see little more than his outline. The orgasm was already building. All intentions to control my sounds fled. I panted and moaned as the euphoria swept through me. I began to shake and then the orgasm ripped me apart.

Andras continued to move, faster and more powerfully, dragging out the pleasure to the point of pain, and I screamed his name. Then he groaned and his movements stuttered. He buried himself inside me, spilling into me.

Tears dripped down my face, getting lost in my hair. Andras leaned down and kissed them away. Then he pulled out, and I expected him to lie next to me, but he left the bed instead. I watched him, afraid for a moment he was going to get dressed and leave, just like all my previous partners. He stepped over the pile of clothes on the floor and went to the washbasin instead, finding a clean cloth and wetting it. Once it was thoroughly wrung out, he brought it back to the bed and poured a glass of water from the pitcher on my table.

"What are you—"

He pulled the pillow out from under my hips and helped me to sit up.

"Drink this." He pressed the glass into my hand and then began to wash between my legs. I gasped and twitched and then settled in as he worked. I sipped the water, realizing only after the water touched my lips how thirsty I was. By the time he was finished, I had drunk the whole glass. He took it from me and refilled it.

"More?"

I shook my head, completely in awe of him. He set the glass on the table where I could reach it and then brought the cloth back to the basin before returning to bed. He pulled the blankets down so I could get under them and slid in next to me, pulling me to him so he could stroke his hands along my back.

"How are you feeling?" he asked.

"Amazing. Exhausted. Awestruck."

He chuckled, the sound rumbling beneath my ear. I traced circles and other random shapes on his chest, just enjoying the feeling of his skin.

"That was intense," I said.

He pressed a kiss to my hair. "Worth the wait?"

"Yes."

He tilted my chin up so I would look at his face. I searched his eyes, wondering if I should tell him how perfect tonight had been, how much I wanted it to continue forever. How much I loved him. He kissed me slowly, the passion quieted but still very much present.

"Sleep, sweetheart," he said, kissing my lips, my nose, my cheek. "I'll be here when you wake up."

My eyes closed. I let the sound of his heartbeat and the feeling of his fingers on my spine soothe me into slumber.

CHAPTER 13

I woke to the sound of a knock on the door and Andras slipping from my side. I murmured a protest, reaching for him, but he stopped me with a soft laugh.

"It's just the brownies with breakfast," he said. He pulled his pants on without doing them up and went to the door. The brownies had already gone, a steaming tray set on a trolley just outside. Andras rolled it into the room.

I sat up and looked from the trolley, then up to him, then back to the trolley. "That looks like a lot of food," I said.

He handed me a fragrant muffin loaded with raspberries and strawberries. I took it.

"Looks like enough for two," he said.

Panic clawed at my throat at the idea that everyone in the house would know what had happened between us.

"Did you tell them?"

"That I would be here?" He shook his head. "No. I didn't tell the brownies."

"But you did tell someone."

"I had to. Guards aren't allowed on this floor without permission. I told the marshal."

"You told Ronan. Who told Calynn."

"Does it matter who knows?"

I didn't answer. I was sure the trembling in my hands and my wide eyes were answer enough.

"I guess it does," he said softly. "Why does it matter, Nialas? Is it because I'm a lowly mongrel?"

"No! That's not what I—"

"Then what is it?"

I could see in his eyes he thought I was lying. I didn't know what to say to make him believe me. The words raced around my mind too fast for me to grasp and formulate into a response that would give him a satisfactory answer but also protect my heart. I couldn't tell him I was afraid of the whole estate knowing how fast—and how hard—I had fallen for him if he didn't feel the same for me.

He stepped into his boots, leaving them untied and picked up his shirt.

"Andras." I wanted to stand and to stop him, but I was naked and I already felt so exposed. Instead, I wrapped the blanket tighter around me. "I don't—Everything has just happened so fast. I—I'm not—" I cut myself off before I said something foolish like *I'm not used to feeling so cared for* or *I love you.*

Andras dropped his eyes to the floor as though he couldn't stand to look at me. I didn't blame him. He took a deep breath and slowly released it. When his eyes met mine again, I could see nothing but disappointment and hurt in the brown depths.

"I understand," he said, pulling his shirt over his head and not bothering with the three buttons I had undone last night. "I'll leave you then, Lady Nialas." Then he gave me a shallow bow and closed the door softly behind him.

The tears that had gathered started streaming down my face. I pressed my hands to my mouth as I stared after him. It was the only thing I could do to prevent myself from screaming.

CHAPTER 14

After Andras left, I threw on my clothes and fled from the house before encountering anyone else. Not knowing what else to do, I went for a walk. I didn't have any idea where I was going. Land passed under my feet without me noticing until I stopped at a cliff face, confused about where I was. A shadow circled over my head as a scarlet wyvern flew down to greet me.

He chittered at me, but I couldn't hear him over the roaring in my ears. I shook my head at him and then fell to my knees, choking on a sob.

Derecho hopped over to me and nuzzled me with his head. I wrapped my arms around his neck and cried. How had I managed to mess everything up so badly so quickly? I kept seeing the hurt in Andras' eyes before he left, wondering what I could possibly say to make him understand how terrified I was, wondering if he would even let me try to explain.

I don't know how long it took to cry myself out. It could have been a few minutes. It could have been an hour. Eventually, my tears were spent, and I pulled back from my friend.

He chirped.

"No. But I'm sure I'll be okay, eventually."

He chirped again, and I smiled at him, wiping the remaining tears from my face. "You're a good friend, Derecho."

He lifted himself in flight and made his way back to his aerie and I started back to the house. On the way, I heard some distant laughter.

How could anyone be laughing while I felt this heartbroken? How could anyone smile? It was irrational and unreasonable, but I didn't care.

I had to pass the laughter in order to get to the house again, so I continued in that direction. Calynn was in the newly built training ring with Ronan and they were fighting, swords clashing. She spun around him as he tried to strike her, and she laughed again. They moved with such speed and grace and I recalled when I'd tried to fight Calynn at the Queen's ball. How had I ever managed to beat her?

"Nialas," Calynn called, a broad smile on her face. Ronan's smile slipped now he knew they had an audience, but I could still see it in his eyes.

A raging jealousy flooded through me. How could she be so happy when I felt like my heart had been torn from my chest?

"Checking on Derecho and his family?" she asked, coming toward me.

"Yes."

Her gaze roved over me and, not for the first time, I wondered how much she could see of me. She always seemed to look far closer than anyone else.

"You look like you could use some exercise. Get in here."

"Oh, I couldn't—I'm not wearing the proper clothes." I gestured at the day dress I had chosen for the morning.

"So what?" She swung her sword in a couple circles. "I'll take it easy on you. You afraid you'll get dirty?"

She was baiting me on purpose. The challenge in her eyes giving me an excuse to unleash some of the pain tearing me apart inside.

"Or maybe you're scared of me. Scared you won't be able to beat me a second time now I have my focus back."

"I beat you before. I can do it again," I said, not sure if I really believed it.

"Prove it."

I stared at her for another moment before I climbed over the railing and jumped into the arena.

"Swords or hand-to-hand?" she asked.

"I feel like hitting something right now."

She grinned and held her sword out to Ronan without looking at him. He took it and then backed away, giving us room.

We circled each other, guards up. When I threw the first punch toward her, she dodged it easily.

"I should mention," Calynn said with another grin, "I've been practicing hand-to-hand far longer than I've been practicing swordplay."

Yet, she didn't make any moves toward me, letting me attack her each time. Every attempt either missed entirely or barely brushed her.

"You're too fast," I complained.

"I don't think so. You're too slow. You're right about wearing the wrong clothes."

I swung at her again and she spun around me. I took the opportunity to charge her back, wrapping an arm around her shoulders. She bent and stood, twisting her hips and flipping me over her, landing me in the dirt.

I gasped as I tried to pull in a breath, but the wind had been knocked out of me. Calynn crouched next to me, waiting for me to recover.

"How did you do that?" I asked.

"Practice. Wanna learn?"

I nodded, and she helped me up. She showed me the motions, and we practiced a few times. Then I tried in earnest and flipped her over my shoulder.

"Ha! I did it!"

Calynn coughed and laughed at the same time. I helped her up.

She wheezed in a breath. "You sure did. Now for the actual test."

Ronan's arm snaked around my shoulders and I froze.

"Loosen up," Calynn said. "You'll never be able to do it if you're that stiff."

"I'll never be able to do it at all! He's too big. I'm too small." I started to panic. Ronan was an exceptionally large man, a warrior, heavy with muscle. Plus, I'd seen him angry before. He scared me.

Calynn made a motion and Ronan immediately let me go.

"You agree we're the same size?" Calynn asked.

"Yes."

"We are almost exactly the same, body-wise, yes?"

"Yes."

"I've been training longer than you, so I'm maybe five or ten pounds heavier than you. That's it."

"Right."

Ronan moved behind Calynn. His arm came around her shoulders and she gripped him, moving in the way she had shown me, and flipped him over. I felt the air magic she used to cushion his fall, but that was the only magic she used. The rest was pure muscle and ability.

"He's about a foot taller than us, but I still flipped him. The move is meant for shorter people to be able to defend themselves from an attack from bigger people. That's why I showed you that one and not something different."

My heart raced in my chest as Ronan regained his feet.

"Ready to try it?" Calynn asked.

I swallowed hard, but dipped my chin in assent.

Ronan resumed his position behind me and after a couple of deep breaths, I tried the move again. He was a lot heavier than Calynn and the flip wasn't as fluid as it had been before, but he still ended up on the ground, Calynn's air magic softening the fall.

I grinned. "I did it!"

Calynn smiled in response as Ronan stood, dusting himself off.

"If you'll excuse me, ladies," he said.

They shared a heated look, but he didn't kiss her like I thought he would. He just touched her hand and then moved off, leaving me alone with Calynn.

"That was a useful skill," I said, the excitement of my accomplishment fading as the pain I had been feeling rushed back.

"You picked it up fast." She looked at me for a moment and then said, "Want to talk about it?"

"About what?"

"Whatever's hurting you."

"Excuse me?"

"You don't always have to pretend, Nialas."

My heart clenched as she said the same words Andras had said to me. Tears sprang to my eyes, and I blinked rapidly, willing them not to fall. I shook my head.

When I thought I could manage the words, I said, "I don't want to talk about it."

She dipped her head in an acknowledging nod. "If you change your mind..."

I didn't look at her, and she started to walk away. She turned back after only a couple steps. "If you want to practice again, you're welcome to join me. Whatever you want to practice. Sword, hand-to-hand, anything else."

"Anything?"

"Yeah, Nialas. I don't have any interest in standing in the way of people. You want to learn something, learn it. You want to do something, as long as it doesn't hurt someone else, do it. You want to be with someone, as long as they want to be with you..." She shrugged. "You just need to decide what it is you want."

She turned and followed the path Ronan had taken out of the arena, leaving me alone. She made it sound so easy.

CHAPTER 15

In the days after my return, I fell into a routine. Keeping busy didn't allow me to dwell on my heartache. I began each day with a trip to the kitchen for breakfast and treats for the horses and wyverns, exchanging pleasantries with Daric. I visited the horses next and spoke with Bainbridge. We would chat about the care of horses and, on one visit, I promised to loan him a book after Calynn had them brought over from Glacia, which she said she'd do. After the horses, I visited Derecho. Cirrus rarely came down from her nest, preferring to remain with the eggs, but Derecho told me she was happy now that she felt safe again and Cyclone had been showing him some new hunting strategies.

After my morning visits, I would train with Calynn or her guard Sorcha. I always did hand-to-hand with Calynn or swords with Sorcha. After I was sweaty and sore, I cleaned up and changed and then spent the afternoons reading. When I fell into bed in the evenings, I tossed and turned until exhaustion took me, missing the feeling of a hand on my back and a heartbeat under my ear. Then I would wake up with my head pounding and my eyes gritty, because I didn't get enough sleep, and do it all again.

Throughout each day, I would unconsciously search for Andras. I didn't realize I was doing so until I found him walking toward the guards' barracks one morning.

"Hello," I said to him.

He stopped walking but refused to look at me. "Lady Nialas," he said. His detached tone cut through me like a knife.

"How have you been?"

He finally looked at me. "Aren't you worried people will see us together?"

I opened my mouth to respond, but no words came out. I knew I had done this, created this distance between us. What could I say? Other than tell him the truth. But if I did that, it would hurt a million times more when he told me he didn't love me back.

He just waited, and then he stared into the distance again, effectively dismissing me. "If you'll excuse me, Lady, I must go."

"Of course."

He continued walking, and I watched him leave.

I didn't consciously decide to arrive in the same place at the same time the next day, but I did. He hadn't wanted to talk to me the day before, so I didn't force him to when I saw him again, but it became a new part of my routine. Sometimes I would arrive just as he disappeared into the barracks. Sometimes I would get to watch him walk. I never made him speak to me.

After the fourth day of seeing Andras, and the seventh day since he'd left my bedroom, I sat in the solarium, reading, when the brownie children entered. They were talking and laughing.

"Good afternoon, Lady Nialas," they said in unison.

"Good afternoon," I responded. "Are you here to play a game?"

They smiled. The older one, Rylan, I believed his name was, said, "We finished our chores early today and Mama said we could come and play as long as we stayed out of everyone's way. Would you like to join us?"

"That's a generous offer," I said. "I'm going to continue reading, though."

They began their game, and I read, distracted every once in a while by their laughter. It was a pleasant way to be distracted. I couldn't remember hearing children's laughter ever at Queran's estate.

My book sat in my lap as I considered that thought. What made this place different from that one?

As I listened to the children's laughter, I also realized the cook had never spoken to me at any of the places I had lived before. They had always been civil and given me what I'd asked for, but never tried to converse with me. Nor had the stable master. Nor any of the people Queran or our mother Eilidh considered servants.

What was Calynn doing so differently?

I stood and went to the kitchens where Daric was busy preparing food, as usual. He stood at a counter, hands covered in flour as he kneaded a loaf of bread.

"Is there something I can help you with, Lady Nialas?" he asked, pausing his work.

"You worked here before Calynn arrived."

"We did. My family and I."

"Brownies choose a house to serve, not a person."

"That is correct."

"What would happen if you don't like the person who owns the house?"

"We would leave," he answered with a shrug, continuing to knead. "There is nothing holding us here but our desire to work."

"You didn't swear fealty to Calynn when she arrived?"

"She didn't require it. And recently, she rescinded all fealty terms she held."

"But she offers protection. What does she get in return?"

Daric snorted. "Loyalty, Lady Nialas. Freely given."

"What's to stop them from betraying her?"

"Well, many of the daoine sidhe have made a bargain with Miss Calynn. Once that bargain has been resolved..." he paused, considering. "Nothing, I suppose."

"Nothing? So she just trusts them?"

He nodded. "All of us. My family, the marshal, Bainbridge, you." He fixed me with a pointed look.

"But why? A fealty term guarantees loyalty. That's what they're for."

He shrugged again. "I couldn't hazard an answer. You'll have to ask Miss Calynn."

He finished his kneading and then removed a tray of rolls from the oven as I stood there thinking. He handed me one and sent me out of his kitchen. I went outside with my roll, picking at it absently.

I sat on a chair on the back patio, staring at the property stretching beyond the house. There were people everywhere. They chatted and laughed, everyone at ease knowing they wouldn't be reprimanded for simply being happy. Even though guards stood on alert at all times—the Queens' threat looming over Calynn—no one seemed on edge.

She really did have a lot of people who worked for her. None of them had sworn fealty. They were here simply because she trusted them to be here. And they trusted her.

I considered my feelings for Calynn and realized my own hatred, that I had held on to so hard for so long, had disappeared completely. It had been replaced with a grudging respect. I didn't think anyone in the whole Sidhe had created what she was slowly building here. A place where people could be themselves.

A home.

I was still wondering about how Calynn had been able to trust these people enough to build this place when a streak of scarlet crossed my vision. I focused on Derecho as he circled and then landed in front of me, something clutched in his claws.

He chirped a greeting, and I smiled.

"Didn't I already see you today?" I asked.

He chittered and squawked as he told me he'd had another visitor after I'd left. Andras had said he finished the carving and wanted to show it to Derecho. He still didn't know all of Derecho's sounds, but they had communicated well and Andras asked if Derecho could deliver the gift to me.

"To me?"

Derecho hopped forward awkwardly and let go of the thing he was holding. It was the carving of him Andras had been working on, complete and stained red to match Derecho's scales. I picked it up and Derecho continued chirping.

"He wanted me to have it? But why?"

Derecho told me Andras didn't say why. He'd just asked Derecho to deliver it.

I pulled the handkerchief Andras had given me out of my pocket and wrapped the sculpture in it. I held the gifts to my chest.

"I appreciate you bringing it to me, Derecho. I'll treasure these gifts."

***

I brought the sculpture to my room, setting it on my bedside table where I would be able to see it as I fell asleep and first thing when I woke each morning. Maybe having something he made would help me with the sleep I'd been missing.

I wished I could talk to someone about all I was feeling. I'd never been in a place where my emotions were so muddled and I couldn't see clearly.

I huffed a laugh at that thought. If I were talking with Calynn, she'd tell me my anger had always muddled my ability to see clearly. How was my love for Andras any different?

I froze as I realized there *was* someone I could talk to. I just had to trust her. The same way she trusted her people. The same way they trusted her.

Leaving my room, I made my way to the library, where she usually spent the afternoons working if she was here on the estate. I hesitated for just a second before knocking.

"Come in," Calynn called.

I opened the door to find her alone, leaning over her desk with maps spread out in front of her.

"You need something?" she asked, not looking up.

I stepped into the library. Hesitated again, then closed the door.

"I wondered if I could talk to you."

As soon as the door clicked shut, she looked up at me. She motioned to the chair on the other side of her desk.

"What do you want to talk about?"

I chewed on my lip, casting my glance around the room. Calynn waited patiently while I found the words. I'd been thinking so many things over the past few days. Where should I begin?

"You said I owed the debt for my role in the selkie's death. I paid it to you. But the debt didn't belong to you."

Now that I was thinking about it, the debt should have been paid to the selkie's family, not to Calynn.

"No. It didn't," she said quietly.

"So now *you* owe the debt."

"I do."

"Why would you do that?"

She sighed and tapped her pen against her desk a couple times. "It made sense at the time. A few people played a part in Meriel's death. You, Queran, Kai, me." She shook her head. "It made sense to me to have all those debts come down to one person. I figured you and Queran would be more willing to pay me the debt than the Summer selkies."

"Who is Kai?"

She quirked one eyebrow. "Who?"

I blinked, but understood quickly. She wasn't going to tell me who Kai was. At least not yet. "Have you collected all the debts?"

"I have."

I had so many questions. How had Queran paid for his part in Meriel's death? What was Calynn going to do, now that she owed the selkie family, to pay the debt? Why was it so important to Calynn that this be resolved since no one else among the noble daoine sidhe seemed to care about their debts anymore? When had they stopped caring?

I didn't ask these questions, unsure if she would answer any of them. Unsure if any of it mattered.

"You said I could do what I wanted now. Since my debt is paid. If I wanted to stay here, what would you require of me?"

She laughed. "I don't fucking know. I don't know what to do with half the people who come here."

"Yet you keep collecting them. You don't turn any of them away."

"Turn them away and send them back to where they came from? No. I won't do that. Guard shifts are shorter and shorter. They're posted every-fucking-where. Housekeeping staff are spread out so people only have one room in one house to clean per day. And the maids. You used to have maids. You want some?"

It was my turn to laugh. "Just like that?"

"Sure. Everyone wants to be busy, but I don't have enough work for everyone."

"I don't think I need a maid anymore." Which surprised me. If she had offered a couple weeks ago, I would have said yes. But I'd changed. I'd gotten used to dressing myself and doing my own hair. Choosing what I wanted to wear based on what I felt like doing.

"If you want to stay, stay," she said with a shrug. "But I don't know you very well, N. I don't know what you would want to do."

"N?"

"You told me once how Nialas literally means nothing. Queran and Eilidh were dicks to name you that. N could stand for anything."

I reached into my pocket and stroked the handkerchief's embroidery.

I looked down at the edge of Calynn's desk. My heart rate kicked up as I considered what I was going to say next. She probably already knew how I felt. If she didn't, she would as soon as I said this next bit out loud.

"I have some information," I said. I clenched my hand around the handkerchief.

"What information?"

"Andras' father is a changeling."

"Oh?"

I met her gaze. "I hoped you could look into bringing his father here. So they could be together."

She grimaced. "I don't know, N."

"I'll incur the debt. Whatever debt you think fair."

The grimace softened to a sad smile. "There wouldn't be a debt. I just don't know what I can do. I don't know what the rules are around changelings and the fae they work for. If they're indentured or free to move about the Sidhe. But I'll look into it. There's someone I know I can ask." She sighed. "There is another problem, though."

"What?"

"You know I don't spend all my time here. There's another property Ronan owns in the human world. That's where I go when I'm not here. And as I said, I have more people than I know what to do with, so some of them are moving there to help guard that place as well. Andras has requested a transfer to that property."

I couldn't breathe. Calynn continued talking. Something about his father not being able to go to the human world. I couldn't hear her over the roaring in my ears.

"N?" Calynn called me back to this world.

I found her looking at me with concern. Her silver eyes locked onto mine. I felt the stinging of tears threatening to fall, hating how much I was crying lately, but unable to do much about it. "I think I made a mistake."

CHAPTER 16

Calynn led me to the solarium. The brownies had gone off some-where, possibly down to their rooms to bed. It had gotten late while I'd spent the whole day thinking. In place of the brownies, a small woman with short, vibrant hair sat with a book open in her lap, but staring out the window.

"Arial, this is N. N, Arial."

The woman turned to look at us, a smile forming on her face and then disappearing into a look of shock. "Holy fuck. You said you looked alike, but you two are identical."

Calynn flopped onto the couch and propped her booted feet on the table. Quinn bustled in with a couple bottles and some glasses, setting them down.

Arial eyed the alcohol. "Girl talk?" she asked.

"N needs some advice." She looked at me. "Whiskey or wine?"

I sat on the second couch, carefully perching on the edge. "W-whiskey?"

Quinn poured us each a glass and then poured the wine for Arial.

"You going to join us?" Calynn asked her.

I felt a flutter of panic but, to my relief, Quinn shook her head and departed. I could probably talk to Calynn about this, and maybe to Calynn's friend. More than that would be too many.

"Okay, N," Arial said, rubbing her hands together. As she did, I felt the magic gathering within her. "What seems to be the problem?"

I blinked, staring at her. "You're part pixie."

She looked at Calynn, then at me. "Apparently so."

"You're Calynn's friend from the human world. What are you doing here?"

"Learning more about my heritage."

I turned to Calynn. "Why am I telling someone else about my problem?"

Calynn sank deeper into the couch, bringing her tumbler of whiskey with her. "I'm shit at girl talk. Arial's better. And, if I'm right at guessing your problem, Arial has more experience than I do."

She sipped the whiskey and waited expectantly.

I pulled the handkerchief out of my pocket, running my thumb along the embroidery. I thought about telling them how he'd been so kind to me when Queran dismissed me. Or how he'd promised to keep my secret of being able to work magic. Though I probably shouldn't mention that, since it was still a secret. I could mention that he'd ensured I was safe and stayed well on our journey. A journey I was wholly unprepared for. I could mention the sex and how he'd been so attentive and caring and forceful and gentle. In the end, I said nothing and just let the tears fall as they came to my eyes.

"Oh, sweetie," Arial said, standing and wrapping me in a hug. "It'll be all right."

"No, it won't. I ruined everything. I got scared, and I pushed him away and he doesn't even know I love him."

"Well, there's an easy solution to that," Calynn said. She poured more whiskey into her glass and lifted it to her lips. "Tell him."

Arial rolled her eyes as she sat on the couch next to me. "Simple and easy are not the same thing. Have you told anyone *you* loved them lately?"

"I tell you all the time."

Arial rolled her eyes again. "I'm not talking about me. And you don't even have the excuse of not knowing if he loves you back. You're just a coward."

"I am not a coward."

Arial stared Calynn down, one eyebrow raised, and I fought not to smile at the exchange. Until I realized what Arial was saying.

"Wait a second. You know Ronan loves you and you haven't told him you love him back?"

Calynn looked down at her glass, refusing to meet my eyes. "It's complicated."

"Mm-hm," Arial said, her tone turning sarcastic. "Very complicated. What's the problem, Calynn? If you don't love him, maybe you should just let him go. Let him find someone else who *does* love him."

The best friends stared at each other for a long time and I worried for Arial's safety. Calynn looked angry enough to burn her friend to ashes. The scary part was, I knew she could do it. Calynn opened her mouth as if to argue, then snapped her jaw shut with an audible clack. "We're not here to talk about me."

Arial snorted and took a sip of her wine. Then she turned her attention to me. "Why didn't you tell him you love him? And who is him?"

"Andras," Calynn answered. "You haven't met him."

"You know?" I asked, my heart racing.

"You went on a journey with him for a week, come back and lock yourself into your bedroom for a night—not nearly long enough if you ask me—and then you both spend the next few days moping around like love-sick puppies. Of course I know."

"We're *both* acting like love-sick puppies?"

"He asked to be transferred to the human world, N. You think he did that because he wants to see a world without magic in it?"

Fresh tears sprang to my eyes, but I was able to push them back this time. "I didn't tell him because I didn't think he would feel the same way. We've only known each other a few days. Most of that time was away from the pressure of other people."

Calynn nodded as though she understood, staring again into the amber depths of her glass. "The pressure of other people is a hard one. Everyone looking, waiting for it to fail. Waiting for you to fuck it up." She laughed. "Except no one is thinking that. You just think they are." She tipped her glass back and drained it. Then she poured more.

Arial leaned over to me and whispered, "In case you didn't catch it, the *you* in those sentences was Calynn." She shrugged and said at a normal volume. "Unless it's both of you."

I sighed. "It's both of us."

I sipped the whiskey and immediately started hacking.

Calynn laughed at me. "I drink it straight, but you don't have to."

"I'm not sure she should be drinking it at all," Arial said. "What do you want to drink, N? I'm sure we can have it brought in if you don't want whiskey or wine."

"I—I never really thought about it before."

"Never thought about what you like to drink?" Arial asked, clearly confused.

"Never thought about what I wanted. About anything. I always just accepted what was given to me and never asked for more."

"Why not?" Calynn asked, sitting forward.

"No one ever cared if I wanted something different. They just gave me what they thought I wanted. Or what they wanted to give me."

"That's the most horrible thing I've ever heard," Arial said.

Calynn sighed and met my eyes. I knew what she was thinking. My story wasn't the worst out there. Some people had been treated far more horribly than I had been. It wasn't something I had thought much of before arriving here. But seeing how Calynn took in everyone and gave them a home, a place where they could belong, I realized how large my blinders had been. I'd been so consumed with how angry I was at the world, I hadn't seen how the rest of the lesser fae were treated. I had assumed it was the way they were supposed to be treated.

"I have another simple but not easy task for you, then, N," Calynn said. "Figure it out."

"Calynn!" Arial said.

"No." I held up a hand. "She's right. I need to figure out what I want. I've been trying the last few days. I have some ideas."

Someone knocked on the door and Quinn entered with another tray filled with bottles. She set them out on the table with some new glasses. Then she gave Calynn a small smile and retreated.

"Quinn has brought us some other kinds of alcohol," Calynn said. "We're getting trashed tonight. And we're going to find something you like to drink."

She poured me a bubbly, golden liquid and handed me the glass.

"How did she know to bring it?"

"She knows things," Calynn said cryptically. "Try this."

We went through all the kinds of alcohol Calynn had and I settled on a cider. We drank and talked and laughed. I felt more at ease than I had in a long time. It felt almost like I could become friends with these women. Something I had never considered before. I wasn't sure I had even considered my life lacking without friends in it. I had always figured friends were not for me.

Calynn drank at least twice as much as Arial and I, but didn't seem any more drunk than we were when there was another knock on the door.

"No more alcohol," I groaned, dropping my head back against the couch.

Arial giggled and the solarium door opened to reveal Ronan's imposing form. He scanned the room, noting each of us and the empty bottles, and shook his head with a sigh. He marched over to where Calynn sat on the opposite couch, stretched out.

"I think you've had enough, my princess."

"Uh oh," Calynn said. "Am I in trouble?"

He arched an eyebrow at her. "Do you want to be?"

She grinned slyly at him. "Maybe."

He sighed, but I could see the smile he fought. He stepped toward her and heaved her up onto his shoulder.

Calynn laughed as he carried her out of the room. "'Night, N. 'Night, Arial."

I watched them go and then heard Arial sigh.

"I want that."

I blinked at her. "You want Ronan?"

"Don't be dense. I mean, he's gorgeous, don't get me wrong. But no. What they have. Even if Calynn can't get her head out of her ass yet to figure it out, they have something special. I want something like it."

"You're not with anyone?"

"There's someone. I thought maybe..." She shook her head. "I could be wrong."

"Or maybe you've also got your head in your ass. That is a strange thing to say. Why would you have your head in your donkey?"

Arial burst into laughter. I hadn't thought what I said was that funny, but she laughed until tears rolled down her cheeks. "That's not what it means," she said, wiping away the tears.

We talked for a while about the strange human words and phrases I'd heard since Calynn's arrival in the Sidhe. When we finally ran out, Arial looked at me, her smile fading.

"So what are you going to do?"

"I have to tell him how I feel. It's possible he doesn't feel for me what I feel for him. But he should know."

"Why do you think he doesn't feel the same?"

"Why would he?"

Arial didn't say anything for a long moment, as though she was waiting for me to say more. When I didn't, she said, "That's it?"

"I believe he cares about me, but no one has ever loved me before."

She blinked. "That is the stupidest reasoning I've ever heard."

"Excuse me?"

"Just because no one has loved you before—which, I admit, is sad—doesn't mean he can't now. Have you ever loved anyone before?"

"Well, no. I've liked people. Before it could develop further, they would always let me know they didn't feel the same."

"Did Andras ever make you feel that way?"

I considered the question for a moment and allowed it to light a hope in my heart I hadn't known I needed. "He always made me feel... precious. Do you think he might feel the same for me as I do for him?"

"There's only one way to know. Calynn's right. You need to tell him how you feel. Before he leaves the Sidhe."

Chapter 17

"Nialas!"

I was startled awake by someone screaming my name.

I jumped out of bed and rushed to see what was wrong. Calynn was in the common area, tugging on a boot, the other one already on, but untied.

"What's wrong?" I asked, breathless.

"Another egg has been stolen. We have to get to the nest now. They're going to be pissed. Where's Andras? I want the people they're most familiar with."

I looked around me as though he might be standing near—where I wanted him to be—but of course he wasn't.

"He's on shift," Ronan said, coming out of Calynn's room, buttoning up his shirt. "We should bring more than just us four."

Calynn disappeared into her room for a second, coming back with her sword and strapping it around her waist. "We're not going to fight them. If we bring a large force, they'll react."

He nodded, and I rushed into my room to find some shoes and a sweater. We went down the stairs and out the back door, where Andras was standing guard on his regular shift. Ronan stopped to speak with him and the other guard, but Calynn just kept walking. I followed her.

"How do you know an egg has been stolen?" I asked.

Her eyes stared straight ahead. "I just do." Her voice was grim. I'd never seen her like this before. Ronan and Andras jogged to catch up, and we made it to the cliff where Derecho and Cyclone circled above, Cirrus still in her nest crying in chittering sobs.

When Cyclone saw us coming, he landed with an angry screech.

"I know," Calynn called. "I promised you safety. I will fix this. I swear to you."

He chirped and swung his head.

"No. Your place is here with your mate. I will find the creature responsible and bring a stop to this. My home is a place where people should be safe. This is unacceptable. I would ask Derecho for his assistance. But you and your mate should remain here to care for the remaining eggs." She turned toward Ronan. "I want a contingent of guards posted here. While I doubt they'll be able to do anything the wyverns couldn't, hopefully the extra eyes will give the creature pause before it tries again. If it doesn't, they might see something the wyverns miss."

"It will be done."

She turned back to Cyclone. "If you'll excuse us, we'll make a plan and then get started. I'll return to let you know what actions we take."

He chirped and lifted into the air again to see to Cirrus, who still sobbed. Her cries broke my heart, tears stinging my eyes. Someone touched my shoulder, and I turned to find Andras looking at me with concern. He wiped away a tear that had escaped and gestured toward the house. Calynn was already walking in that direction, Derecho and Ronan following her.

Andras and I walked side by side without speaking or touching. I missed his touch so much I ached. The knowledge that he was planning to leave the Sidhe created a heavy weight in my stomach. I found the handkerchief in my sweater pocket and crushed it in my fist to keep from reaching for his hand.

Calynn led us into the library and immediately began to pace.

"It was big," she said. "Whatever it was, it was bigger than the wyverns. And it's not just a predator, though it is that."

Ronan stood at ease by the wall near where Calynn paced. Andras, Derecho, and I stood just inside the door.

"I need proof. I need to find the creature and find out what it's doing with the eggs. It has something to do with the imbalance. I'm certain of it."

The Sidhe was supposed to be a place of balance. I'd heard whispers, people worrying about how imbalanced it had become in the last several centuries. Daoine sidhe had been born without magic that should have belonged to them. In recent years, some had even been born without any magic at all. I'd never let it worry me. I was human, after all. It shouldn't affect me.

Somehow, I understood that it affected Calynn more than the average citizen of the Sidhe. The way she spoke of it, like she was directly responsible for righting it. The way she had insisted I repay my debts. The way she began gathering magic within her now, vast quantities of it, like she would use it all to fix everything that had been broken.

Andras' hand slipped around mine and I squeezed it, not sure what was going to happen. Ronan still stood calmly near her, his arms crossed over his chest. How could he be so at ease when someone was drawing in that much power?

Calynn came to an abrupt halt. "But I can't." She looked at Ronan. "I can't go after this thing. I have too many responsibilities here."

He gave a single nod.

"Son of a fucking bitch. This is exactly why I didn't want to be responsible for all these people. But you all got in here and now I can't—" She scrubbed her hands over her face. "How am I going to fix this? I'm being pulled in so many directions. I don't want anyone to get hurt because of what I have to do."

Her magic built and built like a tsunami cresting or an inferno blazing out of control. Andras took half a step forward and pulled me backward behind him. But Ronan stepped right in Calynn's path and gripped her shoulders, holding tightly. I didn't know how he wasn't incinerated from the magic radiating from her.

"We will figure this out, little changeling. You have people who are capable and willing to help. You don't need to run into every situation and solve it."

"I hate putting people in danger. It should be me going," she said.

He gave her a soft smile. "I remember a time when I said that to you. You were right then, but you're wrong now."

She took a step and wrapped her arms around his waist, resting her head on his chest. The magic drained out of her as she calmed. I watched, distinctly aware my mouth had dropped open at the overt display of love and trust between them. My heart ached with desire to find someone I could share that kind of bond with. My eyes drifted to Andras, who still stood slightly in front of me, ready to protect me from Calynn's magic, even though it would certainly destroy him.

I considered what Arial had said right before we'd gone to bed, only a few hours ago. How thinking he didn't love me simply because no one ever had was stupid.

Everyone seemed to take a collective breath. Then Calynn stepped away from Ronan and turned toward us. She took in how Andras stood in front of me and looked away with regret. Then she shook herself and straightened.

"I assume you're willing to help," she said to me.

"Of course. Anything to help Derecho and his family."

She took a deep breath and closed her eyes.

When she opened them again, she was the Calynn I had come to know, in charge, capable.

"Derecho. Did you see the creature?"

The wyvern chirped and chittered and gave a description of a large creature but had very little in the way of details. He did, however, know which direction the creature had gone.

Then Calynn turned to me. "Your magic. Can you use it to find things?"

I blinked, my heart racing. I looked at Andras, who had also gone pale. "Did you—?"

He shook his head. "I didn't say anything."

Ronan gave him a hard look, and I hoped he wouldn't be in too much trouble for keeping something from his superior. But Calynn waved her hand. "I know, I know. Humans aren't supposed to use magic in the Sidhe. Whatever. Can you use your magic to find things?"

I stared at her for a long moment, my mouth agape once again. I'd never heard of anyone else in the Sidhe who could use their magic to locate what they searched for. "Y-yes. But it works by touch."

"Fuck." She began pacing again. She paced back and forth, but this time, her magic remained in her control.

As I watched her pacing, something clicked into place. "How does yours work?"

"By instinct," she said, confirming my theory. "My instincts tell me the direction I need to take and I go that way."

She'd known about my special ability because she had a similar one. Our magic was connected, somehow. I stepped around Andras, drawing Calynn's attention. She stopped pacing.

"You completed all the Solstice challenges, right?" I asked. "You completed every task."

"I did."

"So all of your elements are internal. Mine are all external. I could also have completed every challenge, but only to the first task—using the elements if they were available for me to manipulate. I'm not as strong as you—I can't create an element from within me or remove them from existence—but I can do everything you can."

Andras gasped behind me and Ronan's eyes widened a fraction. Given how much reaction he often showed, it was a lot.

"If you can use your magic by instinct to find things, I might be able to find the stolen eggs by touching one of the remaining ones."

"It'll only help you if they stay in one place. It's not like you can take the eggs with you, so you'll only have one chance to find out where the creature is located. But it's all we have." She turned to Andras. "I already asked you to go on a journey with her before. If you'd rather sit this one out—"

"I'm going," he stated.

"I thought as much. There's just one more thing. Guardian, if you're listening, I could use some advice."

I was about to ask who she was talking to when a huge cat sidhe appeared on her desk, lying on top of her papers as though it had been there the whole time. Its tail twitched as it regarded us with uncaring yellow eyes. I yelped and stumbled back a step, falling against Andras, who caught me and kept me from landing on my butt.

I had never seen one of the Guardians of the Space Between before, but I had read about them. Of course, the books had all said they were a lot smaller than this cat, but few people had ever seen them, so perhaps the books had it wrong. Or perhaps this Guardian was different. I wanted to both move toward it so I could learn more about it, and back slowly away so it didn't have a chance to maul me.

Calynn turned to it, unfazed by its sudden appearance.

"You said I could create a Way to a place I knew well. I've done a few now. I only have to think it to create the Way."

The cat nodded slowly.

"Can I do the same for a person?"

The cat grinned, and it was one of the scariest things I had seen in my life. I gripped Andras' arm.

"You are learning quickly, changeling princess."

She laughed. "Fuck that. I'm making this shit up as I go along."

She turned her back on the cat, something I would certainly have advised against. "Okay. Here's what we're going to do."

CHAPTER 18

Calynn and I returned to the new cliff and told the wyverns what our intentions were. Cyclone flew me to the aerie, and I approached carefully. Cirrus still cried, though her sobs had subsided.

"I'm going to do what I can to ensure this doesn't happen again," I told her. "May I?"

She shifted, and I touched the eggs, concentrating on what it was I wanted to learn. I closed my eyes, and an image flashed through me, the second stolen egg flying over the tops of the trees. I recognized some of the terrain. Then the egg landed, settled inside a fire with another egg.

I opened my eyes and Cirrus chirped.

"Yes. I think I can find it. I can't promise to bring it back. But I promise I will do everything I can to put an end to this."

We returned to the house, and I ran to my room, grabbing what I needed before I met the others back in the library.

"I know where the eggs are," I said, looking down at the map Calynn had rolled out on her desk. I pointed to a spot within the forest not too far from here. "It shouldn't take more than a day to get there."

Andras checked where I was pointing. "If we leave at first light, we can be there before sunset. We'll have to move quickly. We should be able to get there on horses, which means we can get there even faster."

"I don't want to risk the horses." I swallowed and looked up at Calynn. "I think I know what did this and why."

I set my book on the desk. *Tales on the Wing* written by Keilah.

"I think it's a dragon. And I think it's hoarding eggs."

I flipped to the relevant page and handed the book to Calynn, who read the words aloud.

"Dragons and our cousins become fixated on a single item type. We will hoard that item and guard it jealously. If we are not careful, that fixation can become an addiction. The fixation is always on something of high value, something precious. Though the dragon code declares we must not harm others in pursuit of our hoards. If the item we want belongs to someone else, we may not simply take it, but must instead seek terms agreeable to the current owner. Unless the current owner is killed in the course of self-defense. Then, all their property is forfeit."

She closed the book and stared for a long time at the cover, her finger tracing over the author's name.

"Where did you get this?" she finally asked.

"I bought it a long time ago."

Calynn looked up at me, her eyebrow lifted.

"Right. I forgot. I'm just used to saying that. I stole it."

She pressed her lips together, and I suspected she was suppressing a smile.

"Anyway, when I first found Derecho's egg. I wanted to find something that could help me keep him safe and let him hatch. I needed to learn how to care for him as a hatchling. I was ten years old. I couldn't very well go on an expedition to find his nest, but I could raise him until he could find it himself. My magic led me to this book."

"So you think the creature is a dragon?"

I nodded. "In the vision, I saw the egg that was stolen tonight and the one stolen from before."

"You think it's hoarding eggs."

"It placed the eggs in a fire. According to Keilah, you can keep dragon and wyvern eggs alive indefinitely if you place them in a fire. Doing so will halt their growth. Parents use the tactic if they need to leave their nest for longer than an hour or two. That way, the eggs won't get cold. But it's only ever used for short periods. No more than a day, usually. If the egg is kept in a fire, they remain eggs."

"What is it with this world and the children?" Calynn muttered. "They're fucking innocent. Leave them the fuck alone."

The sudden rage filling the room startled me. I forced myself not to take a step back from her as Ronan moved forward, placing a hand on her shoulder. As soon as he did, she calmed again.

Anam cara. Soul mates. The words floated in my mind as I watched them together.

I shook myself out of my thoughts.

"If I'm right about this," I said, "it's possible this dragon stole Derecho's egg twenty years ago. It flew over Glacia and dropped Derecho's egg. I found it and brought it home."

Calynn tapped her fingers on her desk. "Then it's possible, with this fire trick, the dragon has more than just the two eggs."

"Yes." I took a breath. "And more than just dragon eggs. I feel certain the creature has at least a few kinds. I don't know how they kept them all from hatching, though."

Calynn's fists clenched. She stared at the map. I wondered what she was thinking, but Ronan seemed to know.

"You can't," he said. "You have other responsibilities you must see to first. Nialas will find the hoard and you can help her then."

Calynn looked up at me. "Have you ever used your darkness magic to blend into the shadows?"

"I—No. I didn't know that was possible."

She gestured to everyone else. "You three, out. We have a couple of hours before first light. N and I are going to have a lesson before you leave."

Chapter 19

I didn't know what I'd been expecting when everyone left the library, but it wasn't for Winter's best assassin to appear from the shadows.

I squeaked and stumbled backward like I had when the cat sidhe appeared, but this time, Andras wasn't there to catch me, so I fell against a bookshelf, knocking things to the ground. Derecho chittered on the other side of the door, but Ronan's voice was firm when he told him and Andras they were not to enter the library.

Apparently, everyone could know about Calynn's relationship with the Guardians of the Ways, but not the Dark.

"N, I'd like to introduce you to Kai. Kai, this is N."

"Hi," I said, my voice barely more than a breathy sound.

He tilted his head as he considered me, and I wondered what exactly he was thinking. "You wish me to teach her to use the darkness?"

His voice was deep and terrifying. It wrapped around me in a suffocating darkness.

"She's about to do something dangerous. I want her to have every possible weapon she can to stay safe."

The Dark's eyes cut to Calynn. "She was your enemy."

"She isn't anymore. Like some other people I could mention."

The Dark snorted, a sound I never would have expected to hear from the assassin. Not that I'd ever expected to hear *any* sound from him. In all the times I'd seen him at court, I'd never heard him utter a single word.

He would stand, silent and menacing, and those parties were always a little more subdued than usual.

"You trust too easily."

"That's rich, coming from you."

"You should never have trusted me in the first place."

"And yet here we are." Calynn waved a hand between them. "We're short on time. She has to leave at first light."

"She will not be able to use the magic while the sun is up."

My eyes shot between them as I listened to their argument. How long had they known each other? They seemed to be arguing like people who knew each other well. Like family.

"She's going to find a dragon who has broken the code. Once she's found him, I'm going to open a Way to him, and put a stop to what he's been doing."

This time, he outright laughed at her. "You are going to get yourself killed. Your marshal has agreed to this?"

They stared at each other for a long moment. Finally, she said, "He's stealing eggs, Kai. Babies. I won't let that go. So you're with me or you're not. What's it going to be?"

He rolled his eyes and, for the first time, I noticed the spark of orange in the black orbs. From what I knew of him, he'd only ever had one gift. But that spark proved he now had more magic than anyone realized. I wanted to take another step back, but I was already as far away as I could get.

"You know I stand with you. Even when you are being stupid."

Then he turned his full attention to me, and I shrank in on myself a little.

"You have some darkness magic, do you, human?"

"Her name is Nialas. You can also call her N. Be nice, or else."

He flicked his gaze back to Calynn. She stood with her arms crossed over her chest, one eyebrow raised.

He dipped his chin in acknowledgement, then returned to me.

"Have you used your darkness before?" he asked.

I shook my head. "I've mostly used the major elements. I can only use something if it's there for me to manipulate."

He waved around the room. "There are plenty of shadows here. Pull some to you. Let me see what you can do."

I looked at Calynn, unsure, but she nodded and so I found the shadows within the room and pulled them toward me.

They all came, as I knew they would. My magic was far stronger than anyone might guess. Because it would be a death sentence if anyone found out. Or at least, anyone apart from Calynn and her people.

The Dark dipped his head. "Good. I can work with this. You say we have until first light?"

"I was hoping she could get some more rest, but yeah," Calynn said.

"We will need the time if she is to learn everything she must. Without the ability to create them, I do not think you will be able to learn to walk through them. But you will be able to hide in them. And that is good if you are to stand against a dragon."

He slid his gaze to Calynn.

She rolled her eyes.

"She's not going to be alone. Andras and Derecho are going with her. And I'll meet her tonight."

I knew the Dark still didn't think this was a wise plan, but he showed me how to manipulate the shadows, anyway. Once I got the hang of it, it was easy to wrap myself in them until all anyone could see was a deeper shadow. As the first rays of light touched the sky, the Dark pronounced the lesson complete.

"That is all I can teach you in the time we have. It must be enough."

"It's a useful skill," I said by way of thanking him. You never outright thanked a fae without being put into their debt.

"Though how safe it will keep you, I do not know." With that dire prediction, he turned as though to leave.

"Kai," Calynn stopped him. He turned back, and she looked away. I'd never seen her look this way before, as though she was unsure. "I know I've been asking a lot of you. But I could use your help."

The Dark stared at her. "You want me to risk my life to save some eggs from a dragon? Why would I do this?"

"I don't know why *you* would do it. I only know why *I* am. Because it's the right thing to do. We stand a better chance of success if you come along. I know you haven't wanted to show yourself around my people. And you owe me nothing, so I understand if you don't want to risk it."

"I owe you a lot more than nothing."

She waved her hand in the air. "I already told you there's no debt for that."

"The rest of your guard owe you a year and a day of loyal service for your assistance."

"Yeah, but I helped you before I knew I should bargain. So you got a free gift. Besides, you're f—" She cut herself off and glanced at me. I wondered what she was going to say. He's what? Fae? Of course, he was fae.

He glanced at me as well, and I felt like I was intruding on something.

"I can go," I offered. "I have to gather a few things, anyway."

"No," the Dark said. "I will go." He turned back to Calynn. "I will join you. I have underestimated you many times. Though I fear you may be walking into something tonight much bigger than even you can handle."

He disappeared into the shadows. I felt them move briefly, and then he was gone.

Calynn turned to me. "My relationship with Kai is a little bit…"

"Secret?"

"Kind of. Ronan knows, but he's the only one. It's not really my secret to tell. And I haven't pushed."

"You gave him access to his latent magic, didn't you? Like you've helped your other guards."

At first, I'd been too consumed with my own selfish anger to realize what Calynn had been doing. But it was clear now that I'd been seeing it all along.

"Yeah. He was actually the first person I helped. I didn't know I could. I just knew he was about to kill me and I reacted. I'm pretty good at reacting a little recklessly."

"You helped him while he was trying to kill you?"

She shrugged. "It was the right thing to do. If I'd died because of it, I wouldn't have regretted it." She paused. "Well. Maybe a little bit. Either way, it turned out fine, and now he's my ally."

"So you're allied with the Stag, the Guardians of the Space Between, and the Dark."

She considered my statement. "There's a few others, but yeah."

"And you have more magic than anyone has ever seen. Plus, you can tell when people are lying and apparently open Ways. Don't take offense to this, but… what are you?"

She dropped her head back and laughed. "That is a very good question. If we survive tonight, I'll tell you. Before I do, I should mention, whatever I am, you're connected to me. I'm not like the other fae. Which means you're also not like the other human changelings."

"What does that mean?"

"I don't know, N. But you have way more magic than most humans in this realm. You can do glamour, something no other human can do. You chose to repay your debt rather than escape back to the human world."

"Well. If we're being honest here, I had been planning to try to undermine you while spying for you."

"Of course you were. I expected nothing less. But you've changed. You've grown over these last few weeks. So now I feel comfortable telling you, you may be more fae than human at this point."

CHAPTER 20

As Andras and I set out, Calynn's words kept circling in my mind. *More fae than human.* What might that mean? Most human changelings had extended lives, at least three times longer than a normal human. We all seemed to have the ability to wield magic, though none of us did. I hadn't spent much—or really any—time with other changelings, so I couldn't be certain I knew what they—we—could do.

Calynn had said we could discuss it more when we returned, optimistically assuming we *would* return from our fight with a dragon. But I had to admit, I was terrified about facing the creature. Dragons were the most powerful beings in all the worlds. All magic came from their realm, filtering through the others and dripping into the human world. A few dragons made their home in the Sidhe and one—a dragon priestess—was supposed to live here, keeping watch over the magic and offering aid to any who asked for it. Unfortunately, you had to know where to find her in order to seek that aid.

"Are you worried about this?" I asked Andras after we'd been walking a while. Until this point, we hadn't said anything to each other, the silence between us not exactly awkward, but nor was it comfortable.

"About facing a dragon? Of course. But the princess has a plan. And she has more magic than I've ever seen. So..." He shrugged. "We should be okay?"

He said it like a question. As though he was asking me if he was right.

I couldn't say if he was or not. But his faith in Calynn made me wonder again what he felt toward her. Was it simply the respect I had found growing within me? Or was it more? Insecurity bloomed and an evil thought swept through me, making me wonder if the only reason he'd slept with me had been because of how similar I was to her. It wouldn't be the first time someone had used me for that reason. The thought made my hands shake and my heart hurt.

I'd vowed to tell him I loved him, but there was no way I could tell him now, while we still had this whole night ahead of us. What if I told him and he said he didn't care? I was second-guessing everything I'd decided last night.

So we walked in awkward silence for a while until I said, "You have a lot of confidence in Calynn."

I stared forward, but I saw him glance at me.

"I suppose I do. She's proven to be a capable leader, deserving of respect."

"I'm beginning to see that. She really is someone people can rely on. Someone worthy of respect and love."

Andras sighed. "What are you trying to ask me, Nialas? I know it's something."

I swallowed, but still refused to look at him. "Do you... Nevermind. It's stupid."

He caught my hand and tugged me to a stop, facing him. He searched my eyes, peering deeper than I wanted him.

"You want to know if maybe I have feelings for the princess," he guessed.

"Well, I mean. I look identical to her. So I can understand, if someone wanted her, they could use me to pretend."

"You're serious."

"Of course I am," I said, my anger rising to cover the vulnerability I felt. "It's happened my whole life. My parents. Some of the nobles who wanted a bit of power from them. Everyone I've ever known has looked at me and wanted Calynn instead."

I turned and continued walking before I could see the pity in his eyes. Or worse, the fact that I was right. He caught up to me in a couple of strides.

"Let me make something perfectly clear," he said, falling into step beside me again. "I do not have any interest in Calynn whatsoever. She is my princess and my leader and she has proven herself worthy of both those titles. But, setting aside the fact that I don't know anything about her, she is absolutely terrifying."

"You think she's terrifying?"

"Did you see how, when she was getting worked up, she pulled in that magic? Like it all belonged to her and she would just release it however she saw fit. I've never seen anything like it before."

"She wouldn't ever hurt us."

I didn't know how or why I was so certain.

"I agree. But the potential is there. What if she'd completely lost control? What if Ronan hadn't been there to calm her down? She'd never hurt any of us on purpose. Though she could disintegrate all of us with a thought."

"They're anam cara, aren't they?" I asked.

"She hasn't accepted him. As the more powerful one, she is the one who must take that step. But the only way he could have withstood that much magic is if they are."

"There is quite a distance between their magic levels. I thought you had to be closer in magical ability to find your anam cara."

"That sounds like your father's bias talking. A lot of the nobles think that. It's not true. You love who you love, Nialas. There's no rhyme or reason to it. Besides, no one has the kind of magic Calynn has."

We continued on, awkward silence descending again. He was right. A lot of what I'd previously thought had been based on the biases of my mother and father and the other nobles. It would take some time, but I intended to consider each one of those previously held beliefs and decide if it was something I actually believed or something fed to me by people who didn't deserve to hold the positions of authority they had.

"Speaking of how much magic people have," Andras said, breaking into my thoughts. "You didn't tell me just how much magic *you* actually have."

"Of course I didn't."

"Because you don't trust me."

I spun toward him. At least in this, I could make him understand he was wrong. "That's not true at all. I just didn't want you to have to lie for me any more than you already would have to. If anyone other than Calynn had learned I had magic and you knew and didn't tell them, they would have killed you right after they killed me."

"And not knowing how much magic you had was going to change that?"

"I suppose not. But I didn't keep it from you because I didn't trust you. I just figured the less you knew, the safer you'd be."

"Nialas, I—" Before he could say more, Derecho let out a screech high above and dipped down to where we stood.

He chittered for a moment and then took off again.

"I didn't catch all that," Andras said.

"He said he's picked up the scent of the eggs. They're close by. Come on."

We followed Derecho's path, but the wyvern was much faster than we were and so we lost him as he dove into a mountain cave. I started the climb up and Andras caught my arm.

"Where do you think you're going?"

"I have to see what's up there."

"We're not taking on the dragon by ourselves."

"No. But the more information we have for Calynn and her team when they get here, the better. We should go up, see what's there."

"And hide behind what?"

I smiled. "Let me show you my new trick."

CHAPTER 21

When I first pulled the shadows around us, Andras was so startled he fell right out of them, stumbling to his butt on the ground.

He looked up at the column of shadows I'd pulled around me with something like fear on his face. I dropped the shadows immediately.

"How did you...?"

"I got a lesson from someone adept at darkness magic. A... friend... of Calynn's."

He climbed to his feet and dusted himself off. "Who?"

I bit my lip, not meeting his gaze as I considered what to tell him. The Dark was coming with Calynn tonight, so it would probably be better Andras knew now rather than when he showed up. Right?

Calynn hadn't told anyone except Ronan about her relationship with the Dark. It felt odd that I was so concerned about telling Andras. I'd never been concerned before about spilling someone's secrets if it helped me in some way.

"Nialas?"

I took a breath and looked back at Andras. "I wasn't sure if I should say because Calynn has been keeping it a secret. But she asked him to come tonight, so you should know. The Dark has allied himself with Calynn."

Andras rocked back a step.

"Are you serious? Are you certain?"

"Yes and yes. He is the one who taught me how to use my darkness magic. He may even be able and willing to teach me more."

"The princess is allied with the assassin?"

"She calls him by a name. A real name."

"What is it?"

"Kai."

He shoved his fingers through his hair, looking away, obviously trying to grasp the situation, which admittedly was more than he'd been anticipating. He paced away a few steps and then paced back, his eyes finding mine. Suddenly, he started laughing.

"And you thought I might have feelings for Calynn. You thought I didn't find her completely terrifying. She's allied with the Guardians and the Dark. She is so far above me, I'm not sure I'm even in the same world."

"I mentioned the same thing, actually," I said, folding my hands together in front of me. "I asked her what she was."

"What did she say?"

"That she'd tell me after tonight is over."

He laughed again, shaking his head. Then he nodded and waved me over. "Okay. Do it again. I'm ready this time."

I gathered the shadows around us, and we started toward the cave. "I don't have the control to keep us both covered if you're too far away, I think. You'll have to stick close to me."

"I wasn't planning on leaving your side. I can't exactly defend you if I'm not near you."

I wanted to turn to him, search his eyes to see what emotions were there, if he could possibly feel for me what I felt for him. But with the shadows wrapped around us, I wouldn't be able to see him, anyway.

We entered the cave slowly, trying not to trip over any loose rocks, keeping our breathing shallow to avoid the sounds giving us away. Just because the dragon wouldn't be able to see us didn't mean he wouldn't be able to hear us. I searched for Derecho who had flown in and not flown back out. I hoped he was all right and hadn't tried to attack a dragon on his own.

We stayed close to the wall of the cave, walking in deeper and deeper, the natural darkness thickening enough I almost didn't need the shadows to conceal us. I held them anyway, and when we'd gone some distance in, I was glad because, after a few more steps, a light flared to life, illuminating a huge cavern.

There were eggs everywhere. Some had been broken open, some looked like they had been held in stasis for too long and had died. But many, many others looked like they still lived. They weren't all dragon or wyvern eggs, either. Some were frozen in ice, perhaps kelpie or morgen eggs? There were mounds of dirt I assumed hid eggs from creatures of the earth. Eggs suspended in the air in some kind of swirling vortex that had to be creatures of the air. A golden egg hung suspended in one such vortex, this one mixed with flames. I knew it had to be a phoenix egg.

I pressed my hands to my mouth to keep from crying out at the hundreds of babies that had been stolen, so many of which had been inadvertently killed. Though I couldn't see him, Andras' hand found my shoulder, sliding across it and pulling me into him. He held me as I closed my eyes against the terrible sight. After a few moments, I managed another look, finding the culprit among the hoard of eggs.

He was a large white dragon, with odd, spiky red lines covering much of his body. He slept, curled around a mound of eggs that had been petrified over time. And there, sneaking up on the dragon, his tail barb poised to strike, was Derecho. Andras must have known exactly when I spotted him, because his hand clamped around my mouth before I could do more than take in a breath to call out.

As much as I wanted to bite him and shout to Derecho not to do what he was thinking, I knew Andras was right. So I watched in horrified silence as Derecho crept closer and closer. I grabbed Andras' arm, but didn't pull his hand away. Instead, I held on to him. He pulled my back against his chest as we watched in silence.

Derecho continued his approach, moving past the dragon's tail, walking on his feet and the hand-like tips of his wings. *Why doesn't he just sting him already?* my mind screamed. But he continued until he was right next to the dragon's neck. Too close to those sharp teeth. I shook my head.

Andras leaned down until his lips were right next to my ear.

"If his venom is going to do any good, he must sting in the soft flesh of the dragon's neck," he said, his voice pitched so low I could barely hear him.

Derecho lifted his tail and in a move so fast my eyes could barely track it, he stung and leaped away from the massive dragon. The white beast roared awake, the sound rattling the stones of the cave around us as he searched for the cause of his pain.

The dragon climbed to his feet, spreading his wings and stepping on an egg as he did so. My heart cracked with the sound of the egg's shell breaking. Derecho circled back around toward the dragon, screeching with rage as he dive-bombed the bigger creature's eyes. His beak slashed down, but the dragon turned his head in time before smacking Derecho with one clawed foot.

With Andras' hand still covering my mouth, my scream was muffled. But my magic worked just fine, and I caught my friend as he fell from the air, using a swift wind to fill his wings, letting him fly again. He immediately charged toward the dragon, which made my heart stutter, but there was no stopping the fury of the scarlet wyvern. He screeched again, using his claws this time to try to blind the dragon and failing again when the huge beast opened his mouth wide, trying to chomp down on Derecho's smaller body.

I used wind again to shove Derecho out of the dragon's path and then turned him in the direction of the exit, praying to the Sidhe he would take the hint.

He looked around the cavern and this time, I sent a gentle breeze toward him, pointing to the cave entrance again, silently begging him to get out before he got hurt.

The dragon started toward him, making his own offensive strike. He beat his wings, lifting himself off the ground. The cave wasn't very large, so he couldn't get much more than a few feet into the air. But he was faster on his wings than he was on his feet, and he took off after Derecho, opening his mouth again to eat my friend. This time, I reached for all the strength I could and sent another soft breeze toward Derecho, urging him to leave the cave, while a stronger, heavy wind forced the dragon backward.

Derecho finally adhered to my silent pleas and shot out of the cave faster than my eyes could follow. The white dragon followed, slower, but as inexorably as the sun rising. I wanted to chase after them, but Andras held me back, his hand still over my mouth and his other arm around my waist, trapping me against him.

"Let them get out of the cave first. Then we will follow," he said.

There was little I could do other than what he demanded, short of trying to throw him like I'd learned with Calynn. But she'd never taught me how to get loose when there were two arms around me.

"My priority is keeping you safe, Nialas. Derecho made his choice. He's faster than the dragon, anyway. But Calynn won't be able to open a Way to you if you get yourself killed."

He gradually let his voice rise to a normal volume as the dragon left the cave after Derecho, letting me go as well. I let the shadows I'd been holding fall away and turned to him, burning with anger.

"What if something had happened to Derecho? What if I'd not been able to help him?"

"You did help him. And you stayed safe doing it. I won't feel bad for keeping you safe, Nialas."

I turned away and marched toward the fire holding the two eggs stolen from Cirrus' nest.

"What are you doing now?" Andras asked, following.

"I'm getting these eggs out of here."

"You can't."

"Why not?"

He caught my arm, pulling me to face him again. "He'll notice them missing, which will put him on guard or in a rage. Either way will be bad for the princess and her people. Also, the eggs need to stay warm or else they'll die before you can get them back to their mother. It's still six hours before Calynn arrives. They're safe enough in the flames." He started to reach for me, stopped his movement, and dropped his hand. "Besides, I know you and you won't be content with taking just those two. Wait until Calynn arrives, and I'll help you collect them all."

We'd set up a specific time for Calynn to open a Way to me, and Andras was right, it was still many hours from now. The eggs couldn't survive outside of a fire for that length of time. He was also right that I wanted to save all the eggs, not just these two. I nodded, and we left the cave. I pulled the shadows around us again in case the dragon returned. When we made it outside, he was circling the skies, searching for Derecho. We moved away from the cave entrance to a spot a short distance away where we could watch him and the cave but stay out of his sight when he eventually returned. Also, a spot where I didn't have to hold the shadows around us to keep us hidden. It was under some trees, so we were sheltered from the weather and didn't have to sit in snow. As soon as we were settled, Andras pulled out some paper and a pencil and began to draw.

"What are you doing?" I asked, glancing away from the circling dragon for a moment.

"While going into the cave was foolhardy, you're right. It did give us some good information. I'm drawing a map to give to the princess and the marshal when they arrive."

Darkness descended. Andras finished his drawing. The dragon gave up his search for Derecho and returned to his cave. Finally, my friend found us.

"What were you thinking?" I asked him as he landed.

He chittered his response, telling me how his venom would weaken the dragon.

"I don't care if it would have killed him. Stinging the dragon was a foolish idea."

"Just about as foolish as following the wyvern into the cave blindly," Andras muttered. I chose to ignore him.

Derecho squawked indignantly and then spread his wings, flying up to the branch of the nearest tree and turning his back on me.

I shook my head, staring at him.

"You should get some rest, too," Andras said.

I turned back to him, trying to read his face in the darkness. "I'm not sure I can. I haven't been sleeping well lately."

"Why not?" he asked, concern lacing his voice.

What could I tell him? That I'd become so used to sleeping in his arms that without them, I couldn't seem to sleep at all?

"I just haven't," I said, lamely. "Besides, it's too cold for me to rest."

We hadn't lit a fire since it would give our location away too easily.

"Come over here," he said, holding his arm out.

I hesitated.

"Nialas. You need more rest if you're going to be able to get through the night. I'll keep you warm. Sleep while you can."

"What about you?"

"I don't need as much sleep. I'll be fine until morning."

I stood and moved closer to him, curling up on the ground next to where he sat. He shifted closer until I could rest my head on his leg. Then he pulled off his jacket and draped it over me.

"Won't you be cold?"

"No. I'll be just fine. You don't need to worry about me, Nialas."

"But I do. I worry you'll be tired and cold and get hurt tonight. I don't want you to be hurt."

His hand stroked my hair. My eyes drifted closed, sleep pulling me under.

"I thought you didn't care about me at all."

"Of course I do," I said, my voice fading as sleep claimed me. So I couldn't be sure if I said the next words out loud or just dreamed them. *I love you.*

CHAPTER 22

I woke to the sound of voices.

"I don't know what you think you're doing. You shouldn't even be here," Calynn was saying to someone.

"You're going up against a dragon. I'm coming, too."

"You're fifteen!"

"What's going on?" I asked, sitting up and rubbing my eyes.

"They're arguing about who is going into the cave and who isn't," Andras said.

I handed him back his jacket, and he shrugged into it.

"Who?"

"She came with the marshal, the Dark, and three guards. The boy, Rhys, followed them through the Way."

"Oh no. He can't come with us. He'll be killed." I stood up.

Calynn pointed toward me. "See. Even she says so."

One of the guards spoke up. Ansgar, I believed his name was.

"You trust him as much as any of us. And he's better with the bow than anyone I've seen. He can stay back and shoot from cover."

"We've been in the cave," Andras said, handing the drawn map to Ronan. "This is the layout. Derecho managed to sting him, so he has the wyvern's venom in his system. Hopefully, it will slow him down."

Calynn called up a ball of light and hung it above them, showing me the faces of all the people who she trusted enough to bring with her to stand against a dragon.

Ronan and the Dark—Kai. The three guards, Mada, Ansgar, and Sorcha. And the boy, Rhys.

"He's a white dragon," I said. "Which means he doesn't breathe fire. He breathes ice."

Calynn nodded, listening as she studied the map.

"He also has these strange red lines over his whole body."

Her head shot up, pinning me with her silver gaze, one hand clenched into a fist. "You're sure? The lines are red? Kind of spiky?"

"Yes. How did you know?"

"I've seen it before," she said, in almost a whisper. Her other hand dropped from the map, leaving Ronan holding it.

I realized, startled, she'd dropped her hand because it was shaking.

"Where have you seen it?"

She shook her head.

I wanted to press for more information—if it was something that scared Calynn, maybe we shouldn't be doing this—but Ronan stepped forward and began issuing instructions. He hesitated for a fraction of a second before addressing the Dark and asking him to use his darkness magic against the dragon.

Everyone seemed a little wary of him, except for Calynn who wasn't wary of anything... except spiky red lines.

"What about me?" I asked.

"You've done enough," Calynn said, turning back to me. "You don't have to be involved at all. It'll be safer for you if you wait outside the cave until this is done."

"I know. But I can show Rhys a good place to shoot from. And there are hundreds of eggs in there. While he was fighting with Derecho earlier, he stepped on one. He doesn't seem to care if he crushes them. With the fighting going on, they'll all be in danger. I can get them out of the way."

"If that's what you want to do."

"It is. I'm not the best at fighting. But this I can do. I want to help."

"You're not going to argue with *her* about it?" Rhys asked.

"Don't be a brat," Calynn replied. "I've given up arguing. I've given up thinking I'm the one in charge here. None of you listen to me, anyway."

"If we are going, it should be now," the Dark said to Calynn, his voice making everyone shudder except her and Ronan. "From what I understand of your magic, you will be strongest as this day turns to the next one."

She gave a brief nod. "Let's go then."

The Dark wrapped us all in shadows. However, unlike when I did it, we could still see each other. We moved into the cave and he was even able to keep us all covered as we moved away from each other. His control over the magic was more precise than anyone's I'd ever seen and it made me both more impressed and more terrified of him.

Rhys, Andras, and I moved back to the corner of the cave where we'd hidden before, and I took up the shadows to allow the Dark to focus on whatever he needed. As soon as I did, we lost the ability to see each other. Beside me, Rhys moved, and I assumed he had knocked one of his arrows, waiting for his signal to shoot.

The dragon was sleeping again, curled in the same area where he'd been before. In the darkness, we waited, breathless, for the first move. When it came, I gasped.

Calynn stepped out of the shadows. Alone.

"Hey, you!" she called.

"What does she think she's doing?" I asked in a whisper.

Beside me, Rhys chuckled. "Being Calynn."

The dragon woke, lifting his huge head to look down at her, frosty breath drifting from his nostrils. He climbed laboriously to his feet, moving slower than he had when he went after Derecho. I noticed an angry red and black spot on his neck where Derecho had stung him. I wondered if the venom was helping to slow him down, but there was no way for me to know for certain. As he stood, his body seemed to ripple and between one step and another, he changed, morphing into something resembling a human or daoine sidhe.

"Who are you?" he asked, his voice deep and raspy.

"My name is Calynn. I'm the Stag's champion. And *you* have broken some rules."

The dragon laughed, a chilling sound. "The Stag has no quarrel with me," he said, walking toward Calynn.

Her hand rested on the hilt of her sword, but otherwise, she made no move to stop him.

"The way I understand it, dragons are not allowed to steal to build up their hoards. I know you've stolen a lot of these eggs. Now, I can't be certain you stole all of them without actually touching each one, but I'm willing to go through them and find the ones that don't belong and return them to their rightful owners." She shrugged. "You let me do that and I'll leave without any more punishment. But if you make me take them from you, I will have to put you down."

The dragon laughed again. "*You* are going to put *me* down? There is no world where someone like *you* can take on someone like *me*."

Calynn gave him a smile. "You going to underestimate me?"

"What's to underestimate, puny daoine sidhe. You think you can beat me?"

"I know I can, with a little help from some friends."

As soon as she said the word friends, the cave plunged into total darkness and Rhys let an arrow fly. Somewhere I couldn't see, the dragon roared, a sound that should never have come from the throat of something the size of the humanoid he was.

Chaos ensued. I couldn't see any of it, even after I dropped my own shadows. The Dark's shadows were so thick in the cave, I couldn't see anything beyond the rocks we hid behind. Rhys continued shooting, and I wondered how he didn't hit one of our allies.

"Kai," Calynn shouted. "Now."

He dropped the shadows, and suddenly I could see again. Then I wished I couldn't, as the light from Calynn's sword nearly blinded me. Three arrows stuck out of the dragon's body, blood dripping from a number of wounds all over him, but he didn't look like they were bothering him too much. He was completely distracted as Calynn, Ronan, Sorcha, Mada, and Ansgar fought with him.

"I'm going," I said. I ducked around the rocks and started toward Derecho's sister's eggs in one of the fires at the edge of the cavern. Andras grabbed for me, but I managed to get away before he could pull me back. He followed me as I rushed to the fire and used my magic to douse it. I reached toward the eggs, but Andras grabbed my hands.

"Don't," he said, his eyes shining with concern. "You'll burn yourself."

My heart pounded in my chest from the adrenaline, the fight raging behind us. I nodded and he let me go. I searched the roof of the cave for Derecho and gave a sharp whistle when I saw him.

He dove toward us, chittering in question.

"Take these to your sister," I said, pointing to them.

He chittered again.

"I know they could use you. But Calynn vowed to keep them and their nest safe. Taking these back will keep her oath intact. Go through the Way and you can be back in ten minutes."

He took one in each of his clawed feet and flew off with a screech. I looked around the cavern to find the next eggs.

"I don't know what to do," I said. "There are so many of them."

"Gather the ones you can and bring them back to where Rhys is shooting. They'll be safe there."

I started for the next closest eggs. They should all be safe for a few hours outside of the spells that held them in stasis until I could figure out what to do with them all. I carried the airborne ones first to where Rhys still shot arrows whenever an opportunity presented itself.

After a few minutes, I had about a dozen eggs in a pile next to Rhys. He watched as the pile grew and slowed on his shots, conserving arrows and switching from the offensive to the defensive. Andras followed me to each stasis spell, covering me as I took them apart and brought the eggs back. I swallowed hard and started toward the egg in the center of the cavern, the phoenix egg. The fight had stayed mostly to one side where the dragon had made his bed, but this one was closer to the combatants than any other.

Ansgar was no longer in the battle, having been hurt and dragged away by Mada, who stood near him, ready to defend him. Sorcha was favoring one arm. Even Kai, the Winter assassin, looked like he'd been wounded, with a pinched look around his eyes. Only Calynn and Ronan seemed unscathed.

I crept toward the fight and the phoenix egg, Andras close behind. I had just made it and started pulling apart the fire magic when the dragon roared again. Startled, I turned to see Ronan's longsword sticking out of his side, Ronan having rolled out of the way after impaling the creature.

The dragon roared again as he pulled the sword free, coated in his blood. In what felt like slow motion, he turned toward me, pinning me with an icy blue stare before throwing the sword at me. I watched it fly through the air, straight at my chest, and then I was knocked aside. Andras yelled as the sword struck him in the back instead.

CHAPTER 23

I screamed as he fell, catching him and lowering him to the ground. Sorcha was by my side in a moment, helping me with his weight.

"We cannot remove the sword," she said. "He'll bleed out."

"Can we move him to where Rhys is?"

She cast a glance in the boy's direction and gave me a tight nod.

Together, we dragged him, as carefully as we could, to where Rhys protected the rescued eggs. Andras didn't make any noise as we moved him, clenching his teeth tightly.

As soon as he was behind a rock, sitting up and leaning against it on his left side, Sorcha gave me a grim look. "I must return to the fight."

She left us and Rhys came to our side, pulling open the backpack he'd been wearing. "Here," he said, handing me some strips of cloth. "Stabilize the sword so it doesn't do any more damage."

I took the bandages and looked at him, uncertain what to do. He just rolled his eyes at me and took them back. "Let me."

He worked quickly, binding the sword in place in Andras' right shoulder. It had been thrown so hard it pierced all the way through to his chest.

"Where did you learn to do this?" Andras asked him, his voice weak.

Rhys shrugged. "Grew up on the streets of the village. Took care of a few other kids. You learn how to do all sorts of things."

He pulled another larger bandage from his pack and tied it around Andras' shoulder so his arm rested in a sling.

"Don't move it, and when we get out of here, a good healer should be able to patch you up. And Calynn knows a few really good healers."

"Who?" I asked.

"Ronan's uncle is Sir Anant."

It no longer surprised me Calynn had allied herself with the Winter High Healer. Something eased in my chest. As long as this fight ended with the dragon losing and not our side, Andras would be fine.

Then the tension came roaring back when I heard someone yell and fall. I peeked around the rock to see Calynn standing against the dragon. Ronan stood by her side, weaponless. The Dark had fallen. Sorcha had fallen. Both had been pulled back to where Ansgar sat, Mada—barely standing herself—keeping watch over them.

"I have to help them," I said, rising.

Andras caught my hand, his pain-filled gaze pleading me. "Stay. Don't go out there."

"I have to. Derecho hasn't returned. They can't stand against him for long."

"You'll die if you go out there."

I swallowed, staring at Calynn, Ronan, and the dragon. "Maybe. But if that dragon lives, we'll all die, and he'll just continue what he's been doing. No nest will be safe. And he'll take back all these eggs. I can't stand by and watch that happen." I crouched down in front of him, taking his face between my hands. "Before I go, I need you to understand something. That morning, I wasn't ashamed. I was scared. I love you, Andras. And I was terrified you didn't love me back."

"Well, then, you're stupid."

Rhys laughed beside us.

"Yes. You're probably right." My heart rate picked up, urging me to say words I never thought I'd say. "I love you, Andras," I repeated. "I'm not scared anymore. You challenge me while also keeping me safe. You notice me when no one else has before. You expect me to be better than I was, which makes me want to be better."

"I love you, too, Nialas. I didn't expect to, but you surprised me with your vulnerabilities and your trust. Your loyalty to your friends. And I'm going to need you to come back to me."

My heart eased as something clicked into place and I pressed my lips to his, kissing him hard, feeling more centered than I had in my whole life.

"I'll do my best," I said when I broke the kiss. Then I stood and stepped around the rock.

Calynn and Ronan were locked in battle against the dragon. I had no idea how they were still standing. And as I watched, the dragon threw Ronan aside and suddenly, he wasn't any longer.

Calynn watched Ronan sail through the air, halting his progress with her magic and setting him down near where Rhys kept watch over Andras and the eggs. Then it was just me and her.

I went to her side. She was breathing hard, her sword trembling in her hand.

"Why hasn't he shifted back to dragon form?" I asked.

"I'm going to have to do it," she said, ignoring my question. She stared at the dragon, who just waited for us to make the next move, as though he had all the time in the world.

"Do what?" I asked.

"I'm going to have to take his magic from him."

"Why didn't you do that in the beginning?"

She grimaced. "It feels wrong. He was too strong then, anyway. He might still be too strong. But he's weaker now. Derecho's venom and the wounds we've inflicted are causing him to slow." She looked at me.

"He can't shift back. He doesn't have the energy. I'm just not sure if it's enough."

I glanced at him. He grinned at me with so much malice that I shivered.

"What do you want me to do?"

She searched my face. "I want you to take the injured out of here. I want everyone to be safe."

"Too bad. I'm standing with you."

"Are you through with your chat?" the dragon asked. "Or are you ceding victory to me? As you should have done from the beginning."

"You aren't going to walk out of here," Calynn said to him. She raised her sword again, and it glowed with magic. Without any more discussion, she rushed the dragon, and I called up air to distract him from her charge. She engaged with the dragon, who pulled a sword from nothing—or perhaps from his own body—catching her strike and turning it aside.

As she'd once told me, she hadn't been practicing sword fighting for long. She was better at hand-to-hand, but that would be suicide against a creature as powerful as this dragon.

A screech caught my attention as Derecho flew into the cavern, straight at the dragon, distracting him from Calynn's next attack. Her sword plunged into his shoulder and he yelled, throwing her off him. She slammed against the ground, pulling her sword free with her. I watched as she lay still for a moment, twitching and fighting for consciousness.

"Derecho!" I shouted. "Get the wounded out of here."

He screeched again and started toward the first of the wounded, pulling Sorcha toward the exit.

An arrow flew through the air, but with no fighting to distract the dragon, he caught it, crushing it in his hand. I looked around the cavern, helpless. The dragon advanced toward me.

"Well, human? Will you be running now? As your friends should have done."

I shook my head. "I won't run." My heart pounded in my chest, fear and adrenaline rushing through my veins. "I finally found something worth fighting for. I'll stand here until you kill me."

He grinned. "That can be arranged."

Calynn gained her feet, but the dragon stood right in front of me now.

"You have nothing to defend yourself with. You're practically alone. What can you possibly do to me?"

In a move faster than I could really register, he grabbed me around the shoulders and twisted me, pulling my back against his chest, his hands wrapped around my head.

"Drop your sword or I snap her neck," he said, facing Calynn.

Her silver gaze found mine. Slowly, she nodded, bending down to set her sword on the ground. She held her hands up in a gesture of surrender. But her eyes never left mine, and I saw no defeat in them. She took a step toward us.

"Let my sister go," she said. "You don't have to hurt her."

My heart clenched and warmth rushed through me as she said the word *sister*. Like I mattered to her. Like I really was her sister. Even after everything I'd done.

"You are correct. I do not have to hurt her. Perhaps I just want to. Especially after this insulting display."

Calynn took another step and stopped. She dipped her chin in another nod and I knew exactly what to do. We'd practiced it so many times lately, the move had become muscle memory. I bent and twisted, calling on the earth beneath my feet to give me strength, calling on the air around us to make him lighter. I flipped the dragon over my shoulder. He was much heavier than anyone I'd flipped before, heavier than his body should be, but the motion proved to work yet again. From somewhere deep within me, I found some flora magic and pulled it out, wrapping him in vines, tying him to the floor.

Calynn dropped to her knees by his head, her hands over his chest, and the magic I felt flowing from her was like nothing I'd ever felt. The dragon screamed as his chest turned black. He tried to shift back to his regular form, but he hadn't been able to do it before. With what Calynn was doing now, he had no chance.

Red lines started at her nail beds and began snaking down the backs of her hands in sharp, jagged marks matching the ones covering the dragon's body. Calynn's scream joined the dragon's as she pulled his magic from him. Somewhere on the other side of the cave, I heard Ronan's yell next. She kept pulling.

Tears streamed down her face and the lines grew darker and longer, sliding into her sleeves where I couldn't see them anymore.

She shook her head. "I can't," she screamed. "It's too much. I can't."

"You can," I said. "You have to. He can't be allowed to continue." I placed my hand on her shoulder, offering whatever strength she needed to take from me.

That's when I felt it, too—the horrible sticky magic eating away the dragon's power. It felt like tar sliding along my skin. I dropped to my knees, crying out in pain and sorrow. Another scream joined us, but I couldn't place it as the cavern disappeared from my vision. I couldn't say how long it took, but when the magic finished its work and released me, I fell to the ground and slipped into blissful unconsciousness.

CHAPTER 24

I *picked up the egg and it was stone cold. I sighed sadly and went to put it back down when I felt movement from within.*

I gasped and then smiled. "Stubborn little thing, aren't you?"

I cast a glance around, but no one was about. Cradling the egg against me to try to warm it, I brought it back to my room. The warming pan at the foot of my bed was cool now. I emptied the coals into the fire and gathered new ones, sliding it back into place and snuggling the egg near it.

Then I went to my bookshelf and ran my fingers along the spines.

"Too big for a bird's egg," I said aloud. "Too thick a shell for something from the water." My finger tingled as I touched one of the books and I looked back at the egg. Then I pulled out the tome Dragons and Their Cousins. *I flipped through it, scanning for the section on eggs.*

Dragons and creatures related to them share many similarities when it comes to their offspring. The main differences being the size of their younglings starting from the egg. The shells are hardy to protect from inadvertent falls since, even as eggs, youngling dragons can be very energetic.

I continued reading, becoming more and more convinced I had a dragon egg, or at least a cousin of dragons. Perhaps a drake or wyvern. Unfortunately, I found little to no information on caring for such an egg. I searched through my other books and found one on animal young, though the section on dragons and their kin had even less information than before.

I read through three more books before I ran out. I bit my lip, wondering what to do next. The warming pan would keep for at least another couple of hours, so I checked the egg—already much warmer—and went to the bookstore.

I browsed the shelves, finding few books on dragons, and even fewer that had any useful information. Closing my eyes, I ran my fingers over the spines, letting the feel of them speak to me. I stopped when I felt a tingle and opened my eyes, pulling out a slim book called Tales on the Wing *written by Keilah. I scanned the text, finding it full of useful information. Just as I was about to go to the proprietor, I realized I was in the restricted section of the store. I glanced around before tucking the book into my jacket pocket and moving to another section, pulling out a book at random to purchase.*

It took another three months before the egg hatched, but hatch it did, revealing a scarlet wyvern, his sharp beak breaking through the shell and then eating it, something I understood most wyverns did for the calcium. I watched him grow, feeding him raw meat and eggs.

He was only a month old and barely the size of a raven when one day, I looked up from the tome on wind magic to watch my little wyvern pick up his tail in his beak and spread his wings. He flapped them like he was trying to take off and then marched to the edge of the table.

"Be careful," I warned him. "Your wings are new. They might not hold you yet."

He ignored me and jumped off the table, flapping the wings in a fit of incoordination until he flopped to the floor. I set the book aside and helped him back up. He glared at the floor as though it was personally responsible for his failure. I tapped his little beak.

"Keep trying, little one. You'll get there. I'm reading about winds right now and there's one called a derecho. It can go faster than a hurricane or a tornado. One day, you'll race the derechos and win."

He tilted his head at me and chirped.

"Derecho. I think that's what I'll call you." I set him back on the table and stroked his little head as he leaned into the touch. Then he spread his wings again, and I stepped away. He flapped them and jumped from the table, holding them out as he glided to the floor.

"There you go. It's not exactly flight, but it's a start."

***

I woke suddenly, jerking up from the bed and looking around.

A bunch of beds had been set up in the solarium of Calynn's house. Everyone who had come with us to the dragon's cave was laid out in one except Calynn, who sat on a chair, her knees pulled up, arms wrapped around them, staring blankly ahead.

"Are you okay?" I asked.

She turned to face me. She'd pulled her hands into the sleeves of her leather jacket so I couldn't see if any red lines remained.

"Are you?" she asked.

"I think so?" I sat up, looking over at Andras on my other side. Ronan slept on the far side of Calynn. "Everyone else?"

"They'll all be fine. Sir Anant was here yesterday, with Ronan's sister, Assana. Andras' wound was easily healed. So was everyone else's. I had to convince them Kai wasn't a threat. Otherwise, everything went fine. They're all in healing sleeps right now. You weren't injured. Just drained."

"Then why do you look like someone died?" I asked.

"Because someone did. The dragon."

"There was nothing we could do about that. He wasn't going to stop. It had to be done."

She sighed. "I know that. I just wish I didn't have to do what I did. I can still feel it."

"I felt it, too. When I touched you."

"I'm sorry about that. But if it hadn't been for you, I don't think I would have been able to finish. So thank you."

I felt the magic from her statement bind us together, putting her in my debt. Just a few weeks ago, I would have given anything to have her be in my debt, to have Calynn owe me something. Now, I didn't care.

"That magic you used," I said.

She let one hand slip out of her jacket sleeve. The nail beds were still red, the lines fading to pink.

"He'd let it consume him. I don't know exactly what it is, or who has access to it. But I know it has something to do with the imbalance in the Sidhe."

"It scares you."

She nodded, staring down at her fingers. "I can't let it consume me like it did him. The destruction I could cause."

"You said you'd tell me what you are if we survived."

She huffed a laugh. "I was hoping you'd forget about that." She sighed. "Apparently, my destiny is to fix the Sidhe by destroying it. Then I get to become queen of the whole thing for a while. And finally, the Ancient Mother."

"But... isn't the Ancient Mother supposed to be... ancient?"

She scrubbed both hands over her face. "I don't know, N. All I know is what she told me and what I've been able to piece together. She wants me to do one thing. Something else wants me to do another. Whatever that something else is, it doesn't exactly have a voice, so it can't just tell me what it wants. I'm stuck trying to figure it out on my own. And I've only known about this place for a few months. How am I supposed to figure anything out?"

"Well, you have time. Don't you?"

She wrapped her arms around her knees again and laid her head on them, looking at me. "No. Another few months. That's it."

I thought about it for a moment. "The Spring Equinox."

"Mm-hm. Our birthday."

"That seems like quite a coincidence," I said slowly, not certain I really believed it was one.

"I don't think it is. I'm pretty sure it was all designed this way for a purpose. Well, except the changeling part. You just get to be part of it because Queran made a choice and then Ronan made another one. I'm sorry about that, too."

"Stop apologizing to me," I snapped. "I don't want your debt. I want to help you."

"Why?"

"Because there are creatures here who don't deserve to be destroyed. I think that's what's causing your doubt in this whole thing as well. You want to help people. You want to do the right thing. I know you'll figure out what it is. And when you do, I'll stand with you. Even though I'm just a human and I don't know how much I can offer you, I'll stand with you."

She smiled. "You're fae enough to have an anam cara."

My gaze shot to Andras, who still slept in the bed next to mine. "What? How?"

I looked back at her, and she lifted her head and shrugged. "I don't know. I felt it when you offered me your strength. When you did that, you accidentally offered his, as well. I tried not to take too much from him since he was already injured. But I needed a little."

"He'll be all right?"

"Yeah. Just a little tired like you. Besides, where did you think those vines came from you tied the dragon down with?"

"I just assumed there had been some there somewhere."

"No. It came from inside you. Or rather, inside Andras and then through you."

"I can use his magic?"

"The same way he can use yours. Your magic is connected now. It goes both ways."

"Can Ronan..." I trailed off, not sure if I should be asking the question.

"I don't know. He never has. I haven't quite figured out what makes two people become anam cara. When I do, I'll let you know."

CHAPTER 25

Quinn brought me books to read, but she and Calynn refused to allow me out of bed for anything other than relieving myself. Daric brought me food, and I settled in to wait as the rest of the group woke up. The only person, other than Calynn, who hadn't needed healing was Rhys. He stopped by to say hello and ask how I was feeling. He told me the wyverns had taken all the eggs I had gathered out of the cave and brought them back here. People were helping to figure out what kinds of eggs they were and how to care for them. I asked for them to be brought in with all the books from the library that might help us identify them.

With Rhys' help, I found out what they all were and set tasks for how to care for each one until I was allowed to take over the care myself. I made a plan to return to the cave and check the remaining eggs I hadn't been able to free from the stasis spells. Calynn had assured me the spells hadn't dissipated with the dragon's death.

Ronan was the next to wake. Unlike me, he refused to listen to the healer's orders and got up right away. Calynn went with him and I noticed how she clung to his hand and how he clung to hers as they left the solarium.

The Dark woke in the middle of the night. He sat up in bed, looked directly at me, gave me a shallow nod, and disappeared into the shadows.

I slept, and when I woke the next morning, Sorcha, Ansgar, and Mada had all woken as well and were eating breakfast.

Calynn came to check on everyone and pronounced anyone who wanted to leave may do so. The three guards left, but I remained.

"He'll wake soon. Anant said either today or tomorrow. He was the most hurt. And with the strength I took on top of that..." she trailed off and I could see the regret on her face.

"I'm certain he would have wanted you to take it. If it meant stopping the dragon."

She shook her head. "It doesn't matter. You offered your strength. He didn't offer his."

She sat with me for a while. We talked about what I could do since I'd decided to stay and I didn't want to be idle. Eventually, she had other things to see to and left.

I was just thinking about sleep when Andras stirred.

I watched, my breath held in my lungs as I waited to see if he would wake.

When his eyes blinked open, I dropped to the floor on my knees beside his bed, placing my hand over his.

"Hi," I said.

He turned to look at me, his look of confusion changing to one of relief and then anger.

He sat up—much faster than the healers probably would have let him, had any been around—and grabbed me by the shoulders.

"What were you thinking? He could have killed you. And you just stood there like you were going to take him on single-handed. You nearly gave me a heart attack."

I pushed on his shoulder, the one that had recently had a sword impaled in it. "Same," I countered.

His grip shifted until he pulled me to him, crushing me against his chest. "Don't do anything so dangerous again. Please. I'm begging you."

The fae never said please or thank you or I'm sorry. Over the past couple of days, I'd heard those words more than in the rest of my life combined.

My arms wound around him, anchoring me to him. "I don't think I can promise that right now. Not with what Calynn told me is coming. But I can promise you whatever dangerous thing I do, I'll do it by your side if you let me."

"I wouldn't have you anywhere else."

I sat on the edge of his bed, sitting back from him a bit so I could see his face.

"I need to tell you something," I said.

"The look on your face tells me you don't think I'm going to like this."

"I don't know. In the cavern, when Calynn was pulling the magic from the dragon, she was struggling and I offered her my strength. When I did that, I inadvertently offered her yours as well. Somehow, even though I'm human, Calynn believes we are anam cara."

He reached a hand up to stroke my cheek, tucking a loose strand of hair behind my ear, then trailing his fingers down my spine in that familiar caress that always put me at ease.

"I don't know how it happened and I don't know if you even wanted it to happen. I know what we said in the cave, but just because you may be in love with me now doesn't mean you think you're going to love me forever."

I bit my lip to keep from saying any more.

"Are you finished, then?" he asked.

"I guess so?"

"Good." Then he kissed me, drawing me back toward him, sliding his tongue between my lips to caress mine. I kissed him back, my fingers tangling in his hair, my body thrumming with need.

He drew back, planting soft kisses on the corners of my lips and my nose and forehead as he did so.

"I don't know how it happened, either, but I'm glad it did. You're smart and funny and beautiful. You're loyal and kind."

"I'm not kind. Or I haven't been."

"You are kind to those who you believe deserve kindness. You just didn't think some people did. But you're also willing to learn from your mistakes, and that is not something I've seen in many people. If Calynn had needed all my strength, and it kept you safe, I would have given her everything. Nialas, you can have everything in me. As much or as little as you want for as long as you want. Including forever."

My heart ached with the love I felt for him and from him. Then I noticed something else I felt from him: exhaustion. I urged him to lie down and then quickly got up to shove my bed next to his. I climbed in and we held each other in the dark and quiet of the house.

"I've been thinking of something else lately," I said. "Since I woke up, actually."

"What's that, my love?"

My heart swelled at the endearment.

"Did you know I gave Derecho his name? He was just a little thing then, just learning to fly."

"So you named him after a wind?"

"It seemed fitting. I don't think I've ever mentioned to you how much I hate my name."

"You haven't. But I can guess why." His fingers drifted up and down my spine. I drew patterns on his chest with my own. "No one would like being named nothing."

"I've been thinking, if I could give Derecho a name, perhaps I can give myself one, too. Calynn nicknamed me N, and I like that. But N is just a letter."

"And you want a name. What about Niall? It's close to Nialas so no one should have difficulty adjusting. And, while it is usually a male name, I think its meaning fits you well."

"What does it mean?" I met his eyes.

"It means champion. After that fight, you have certainly earned that title."

"Are you trying to get me to fall in love with you again?" I asked.

He smiled and kissed my forehead. "I would have you fall in love with me every day for the rest of our lives."

"You're not afraid I might live a much shorter lifespan than you?"

He shook his head. "Whatever is mine is yours, my love. My magic, my lifespan, my heart. Have it all."

"Only if you have all mine."

EPILOGUE

I t took another day, but eventually, Andras and I returned to the cave with a small contingent of guards. I wasn't sure how many of the eggs we would need to carry and didn't want to make any more trips than I had to.

I moved around the cave, bringing forth some light from outside to brighten the dank space. I went from egg to egg, checking to see which were still alive and which were not. We'd originally brought fourteen to Calynn's property, and I found another twenty still alive in the cave, including the one in the center, the only phoenix egg in the collection.

The stasis spell on the phoenix egg was the most difficult to undo. I'd sent all the guards back to Calynn's estate already with the other eggs, so now it was just me and Andras, trying to free the last one.

"I've been doing research on them," I said as I pulled the fire from the spell, leaving the egg in a vortex of air. "Phoenixes don't lay many eggs. Usually one every hundred or so years." I slowed the vortex until it was little more than a light wind keeping the egg aloft. "And it takes them another hundred years to hatch. The phoenix doesn't brood the egg. She just leaves it and it hatches in its own time, but it needs to hatch from a pile of embers."

"What happens if there are no embers around when it's time to hatch?"

"Then the bird that emerges will not be a phoenix."

"After waiting a hundred years, and it won't even be a phoenix?"

I shook my head, reaching out and carefully removing the egg from the air. As soon as I touched it, I felt the movement from within. A tiny beak pressing against the shell.

"It's trying to hatch," I said. "Quickly! We must build a fire."

Since my magic required the presence of the element, Calynn suggested I carry a vial of water, a leaf, some flakes of metal, and a few matches. I took one out, striking it against the rocks. The vines I had grown to trap the dragon were still there, though he had long since disintegrated. I lit them on fire and Andras ran out of the cave and brought back some neatly cut logs faster than anyone without flora magic could have done. He set one on the fire and then another. I continued feeding it magic until I thought the logs had burned enough and then I doused it, leaving only the embers behind. Then I set the egg in them and we waited.

It took about half an hour for the bird inside to break free from its shell, making little chirping noises as it did so. Finally, it was free and as soon as it left the shell and touched the embers, it burst into flame. Andras stumbled back a step, but I just leaned closer.

"That's right, little one. You can't become who you were meant to be without walking through the fire."

The ashes fluttered down to mix with the embers. They stirred around and around as though in a draft, though there was no wind in the cavern. After another thirty minutes of watching, a tiny head poked out of the cooling embers.

"There you are," I said, holding out my hand. "It's nice to meet you. You certainly had a rough time of it, didn't you?"

The tiny bird fit in the palm of my hand, his feathers a dull gray the color of ashes.

"But you're here now, and that's all that matters."

I turned and showed him to Andras who waited just behind me.

"What are you going to call him?" he asked.

"I'm not sure yet. You have to get to know someone before you can give them a name."

The End

If you enjoyed *Out of the Embers*, please consider leaving a review. Reviews help indie authors like me gain exposure which helps sell books. Which helps me create more books.

Have you read the other Glamour Blind books yet? Calynn's books are available to read, so what are you waiting for? You can find them wherever you like to buy your books.

In *Truth in the Smoke*, Calynn learns she's not as human as she thought she was and begins a search for the truth that leads to breaking and entering, an assassin, and a man with more than a few secrets of his own.

In *Destiny in the Flames*, Calynn didn't really like the last answers she found, but now she's on the hunt for some more. What is her destiny and how is it connected to dreams of shattered windows and a mysterious, faceless woman?

But you should have already read those books, and now you want to read the last one. Turn the page for a sneak peak at the first scene of *Hope in the Inferno*.

Hope in the Inferno

When I woke up in the middle of the night, Ronan was no longer sleeping beside me. This didn't worry me since he often kept odd hours as my marshal, the head of my guard. I got up and dressed in black pants, a black shirt, and my black leather jacket and riding boots. Then I let the shadows in the room envelop me and I moved through them out of the house and across the property.

I'd been practicing the magic since my return to the human world from the Sidhe. My cousin, Kai, had been teaching me. And now I understood why he wore all black clothing. Well, maybe for him, it was a style choice to go with his black skin and eyes, but for me, it made it easier to blend into the shadows.

I appeared next to the Way to Winter, where Kai and I had agreed to meet, and stepped out of the darkness. Instead of a shadow among shadows, I found myself surrounded by guards, weapons drawn and pointed at me.

"What are you doing here?" Ronan asked as he casually stepped into the circle.

"A little melodramatic, don't you think?" I responded.

He closed his eyes in a bid for patience—I'd seen the look enough times before to know what it meant.

Then he opened his eyes and said, "My princess, how am I supposed to protect you if I don't know where you are?"

Kai appeared next to me as though from thin air. "Are we going to fight your personal guard?" he asked curiously.

A few of the people gasped and stumbled backward. They must be new, since most people had gotten used to him appearing from nowhere.

"I don't think that's going to be necessary," I said, staring hard at Ronan.

He jerked his head in a dismissive gesture, and the guards put away their weapons, falling back. I noticed Ansgar and Mada in the group, as I expected, and they took charge of the others, leading them away. Once we were alone except for Kai, Ronan fixed me with a stare.

"Don't bother trying to tell me this is the first time you've gone wherever you're going," Ronan began, stalking toward me in a way that might be menacing to anyone else. Especially with his naked sword held against his shoulder and how much taller he was than me.

I felt a tingle run down my spine, but it wasn't fear. He was very hot when he was in charge.

"I wouldn't insult you like that."

"So just where have you been going?"

"Well, you know how we've added a few more to our numbers lately and they all look a little..."

"Ragged?" Kai supplied.

"Tortured," Ronan said. "Ancient Mother be merciful. Little changeling, tell me you haven't been sneaking into the Queen's dungeon and freeing prisoners."

"Okay. I haven't been sneaking into the Queen's dungeon and freeing prisoners."

He closed his eyes again, this time to hide the emotions I could always see in them.

"You take too many risks," he said.

"You've said that before. You'd think you'd be used to it by now."

His eyes flew open as he gripped my shoulders, just shy of the point of pain. "I will never get used to you being in danger."

And there it was, everything he had been trying to hide. The fear for my safety. The frustration that he couldn't stop me. And the love.

"You know I need to do this," I said, touching his cheek. "After what happened to you, and to the person who failed the flora challenge..." I shuddered as I recalled the man completely broken by the Queen in a matter of hours. His empty expression as she led him around on a leash before handing him back to his family. "Do you really think I can stand by and let that continue to happen?"

He didn't let go of me. "You also have obligations *here* you have to take care of."

There were certainly a lot of things I'd been putting off lately. All of them big decisions that I didn't want to deal with. The responsibility of so many lives weighed heavily on my shoulders. I couldn't run from that responsibility, but I could focus on something else for a while. "I know. And I will. But I also need to do this."

"Then let me come with you."

"You don't have any darkness magic. Kai and I can get in and out fast. Besides that..." I hesitated, recalling what the Queen had said when I rescued Ronan from her torture chamber. Words he hadn't heard because he was so deep in the abyss that had kept his mind intact during weeks of pain. *You must be careful with your toys. Because next time, I* will *break him. If only because I now know how important he is to you.* "You've spent enough time in her dungeons."

He leaned his forehead against mine. "You make things so difficult."

The side of my mouth hitched up in a semblance of a smile. "Always."

"If we are to go, it must be now," Kai said. "Or else we will not have the time we need."

I raised an eyebrow at Ronan, waiting.

"You know I won't stand in the way of something you believe you must do. Nor can I stand idly by while you do something foolish just to prove a point." He glanced at Kai then back at me. Then he let me go and stepped away. "Just come back."

"I will."

I wanted to kiss him, but he never kissed me in front of people. And from what I understood, that would be a declaration I wasn't quite ready to make. So I stepped away and followed Kai through the Way.

I'd created it a bit more than a month ago, opening a Way directly from my estate to Ronan's ranch to ensure I could come and go between the two without difficulty and in relative safety. To ensure no one tried to come onto his property, I also closed the Way that had originally led from his ranch to a spot just north of Glacia.

Once we were in Winter, Kai placed a hand on my shoulder. He had been to the Queen's dungeons more than I had and knew the shadows there better.

As we slipped into the darkness, I said, "I know. I should have told him where I was going. But I didn't want him worrying. I've caused him enough grief over the years, don't you think? And considering he's in love with me, and I haven't figured out if I'm in love with him, it's hardly the worst thing I've done to him, right? But really, who falls in love with someone after only a few months? It's just not reasonable to think someone could fall in love that fast. Right?"

"Calynn," Kai interrupted my rambling.

I held my breath, waiting for some profound piece of wisdom from the depth of his thousand years of life experience.

"You're asking the wrong person," he said.

"Oh." I paused, considering. "You mean, you haven't ever fallen in love? Not even a little bit?"

He shot me a look, one black eyebrow cocked. "I've spent my life as an assassin. My queen turned me into someone to be feared, not loved."

I set my teeth together, adding one more thing Mab would have to pay for to her ever-growing list of debts.

Before I could respond, we stepped out of the shadows into the lowest level of the dungeons. When I'd first brought up the idea of freeing prisoners after a little foray into a dragon's den to free some stolen eggs, Kai had told me about this place. It was where Mab stored the prisoners who she had finished torturing, but didn't want to release yet. Some people we had released had been there for centuries. They had been left forgotten, not even a guard to watch them, only fed once a week—just enough to last them if they rationed properly.

Tonight was feeding night.

Over the last week, we had taken them to my property in Winter or Ronan's ranch in the human world. Tonight, we would liberate the final two prisoners before the guard brought food at dawn. Kai took up a spot near the stairs to ensure we weren't disturbed, and I moved to the last cells at the very back of the dungeon. I peeked in through the window, but couldn't see anything in the shadows.

"Hello?" I called quietly.

Something rustled inside, but there was no other response.

"Is anyone in there?"

Still nothing. I cast a glance at Kai who gave me a look that told me to hurry. I nodded toward the cell and then wrapped myself in shadows, stepping out on the other side of the door so I was inside the cell with the prisoner. After I was inside, it occurred to me I should maybe have been a little more careful. Especially when the prisoner screamed and launched herself at me, fingers extended as though she wanted to claw my eyes out.

Thankfully, I'd been practicing krav maga for the past ten years and I caught her as she attacked and threw her against the wall.

"Now that's not a very nice way to greet the person who is here to get you out of this shit-hole."

It had been easy to throw her. She was little more than skin and bones. Even so, she looked up at me from the floor, murder in her dark eyes. With her back pressed against the stone, she got carefully to her feet. I could feel her calling on her magic. The air crackled with electricity as sparks of it traced through her pure white hair. I called upon the magic from the earth, grounding the lightning before she could hurl it at me and then stepped into the shadows again. She twirled around, seeking me, but I'd learned darkness magic from the best and she had none of it herself. I stepped out of the shadows behind her, wrapping her in a choke hold.

"If you're not going to play nice, neither am I," I said, holding the choke for the few seconds required for her to slump against me, unconscious. I lay her gently on the ground, quickly tying her hands and feet together with the zip-ties I'd packed along in case we ran into a guard. Tonight, I didn't have time to play games with the prisoner. I found a bandana in another pocket and tied it around her mouth so she couldn't scream, and then pulled her with me into the shadows, moving to the other side of the door where Kai waited.

"We are out of time," he said, glancing at the girl. "They are coming down the stairs now."

"But you said they bring the food at dawn. That's still another hour."

"They are early tonight."

"Son of a fucking bitch."

"We must leave before we're found."

I stood my ground. "I'm not leaving the last prisoner."

"Our only other choice would be to kill the guard. You said you did not want to do that."

"I don't. And I won't. The guard is innocent in this. He's just following orders."

Well, most of the guards, anyway. And I wasn't going to take the chance on guessing this person's status.

I could hear the steps on the stairs now. He would be here in a few seconds.

"Take the girl," I said.

Kai blinked at me.

"Take her. I'll get the last prisoner and meet you at the edge of the city. I should be able to get that far on my own."

Kai bent to pick up the girl, hoisting her over his shoulders as she started to stir. She was going to be a fight when she came to, but Kai would deal with it.

"Your lover will not like you staying behind on your own," Kai warned me. Then he disappeared into the shadows before I could respond.

I glared at the spot he had been for only a second before I also pulled the darkness close and let it carry me to the other side of the dungeon and into the final cell. The guard descended the steps as I looked out, still cloaked in darkness. He carried a couple loaves of bread and a bucket of something that looked like congealed oatmeal. He set the bucket down and went to the door of each cell, collecting the bowls that I had made sure were placed at the small flaps where he'd expect them to be. As he came closer to the cell I was in, I held my breath until he moved away back to a table where he ladled sloppy goop into each bowl. He wouldn't be long. I turned to find the prisoner and almost mistook him for a pile of rags in the corner. He was tiny, his head resting on his knees, eyes closed. As I inched closer to him, I realized he was a child. He was a child like Rhys.

Fagen. There was no mistaking it.

He was thirteen and had been Rhys' best friend. We'd all thought he'd been killed when Queen Mab had tried to eradicate the chalice children from the village. But here he was. Alive.

Every single prisoner I'd helped free had made some kind of noise when I appeared in their cell. I had to somehow get Fagen to come with me, silently, in the next two minutes before the guard opened the first door.

I eased the shadows away from me, letting myself appear in the room slowly so as not to startle him. Then I crouched in front of him, one finger pressed against my lips in a bid for silence. I touched his shoulder.

He jerked upright with a gasp. But he took my warning and stayed otherwise quiet.

"We have to leave now," I said in a low whisper.

He nodded and stood, taking my outstretched hand. Just as his fingers touched mine, the guard opened the first cell.

I pulled the boy against me and wrapped us both in the shadows, slipping into the corner of the room. Unlike Kai, I couldn't just think of where I wanted to go and have the darkness take me there. I had to see where I was going. Though I could move much faster in the shadows, I still needed a line-of-sight to get there. This dungeon was underground, so there were no windows I could look through to get outside the palace.

The guard sounded an alarm, and I could hear people rushing down the stairs. They would check every cell, but they wouldn't be able to see us unless they brought enough light to dispel all the darkness. We stayed huddled in the corner, waiting. Finally, a guard flung the door open and I could see where everyone stood in the main room. There were five more guards, all opening cells, searching for prisoners who were no longer there.

I held the boy tight as I moved through the shadows to the far side of the room, waiting for the set of boots on the stairs to come down before starting up. I wasn't certain if someone bumped into me if they would feel me, so I decided not to risk it. Wouldn't Ronan be proud? Every time I heard more guards coming, and there were a lot of them, I pressed the boy and myself against a wall and held my breath until they passed.

We made it up to the next level of the dungeons—where Mab did all of her torturing—but it was underground as well. I had to get up one more floor before I could find my way out. I was about to continue up when I heard a familiar voice and the boy in my arms began to tremble.

"What do you mean gone?" Mab said.

"All of the cells are empty, Your Majesty. The doors were closed and still locked. The bowls were at the flaps, just as they should be. But when he opened the doors, no one was inside."

I couldn't see her. She was inside one of the torture rooms, the door standing open. Light flooded out and I could see a couple of shadows, Mab's and whoever was talking to her. A whip cracked and someone screamed. Fagen trembled harder, tears leaking into my shirt where his face pressed against me. I swallowed as I listened to the consequences of my actions. Mab was pissed. And she would take her anger out on whomever was in that room with her—if not others as well. I clutched Fagen. I had saved him, and another fifteen people. But what would the final cost be?

I forced my feet to move, to carry us—cloaked in darkness—one more level up. It took a lot longer as I did my best to avoid the torches casting light that ate up the shadows I moved through. But I reached the ground level and found a window with a clear sight line to the other side of the river, all the way down the road that would take us out of the city. I gripped Fagen tighter and moved through the shadows faster than I had ever moved before, getting us outside the gate and beyond the small town on the far side. We continued toward the Way, Kai finding us during our sprint; he added his shadows to mine, helping me move faster until we were safely away and back in the human world.

Something Ronan had once said floated back to me through my memory. *Each action has a consequence, sometimes ones that are far more terrible than doing nothing in the first place.* I couldn't believe that was true in this case. But the sound of that scream would haunt my dreams for a very long time.

ACKNOWLEDGEMENTS

I didn't mean to write this book. If I'm being honest, I don't actually remember starting it. I've been working so fast on so many stories lately, it's all blurring together. But I know the intention had been to write something short to give away to newsletter subscribers. But then Nialas started becoming something more than what she had been before and what was supposed to be a short story became a novella. And here we are.

So, here come the thanks, because, though people may believe that writing is a solitary activity, it really is not.

As always, my first thank you goes to my Team Hikes and Games: Krys, Steph, Jenn, Meagan, and Kim. You guys are the absolute best friends a person could as for. I know my questions might get annoying sometimes, but you answer them as though they aren't.

Thank you to my editor, Tracy. Your feedback is both helpful in terms of making the story better and helpful in letting me know I'm actually maybe kind of good at this writing thing. So thank you.

To my beta readers, Krys, Colleen, and Ashley. Thanks for all the little things you caught. And for the slightly bigger things as well. That dragon really needed to shift before he started talking.

Thank you to all my writing friends at Blood and Pulp, The Creative Academy for Writers, and Author Ever After. If you are an aspiring writer and want a free piece of advice, it would be this: find a writing community. The support and friendship I have found in mine have been invaluable.

Last but not least, thank you to Sean and Ryan for all of your patience and tolerance when I'm spending too much time at my laptop. Love you guys.

About the author

SP Neeson's recipes for books always include a little bit of twisted tropes, a handful of found families, and a dash of swearing and spice.

She also writes contemporary romance under the pen name Sarah Neeson where you can find more delicious stories but in a contemporary setting.

When she's not writing, she can be found having fun with her family or hanging out with her angora goats.

And yes, the u in "favourite" means she's Canadian.

Follow Sarah on Facebook and Instagram @sarahneesonwrites

Manufactured by Amazon.ca
Bolton, ON